Taylor Smart
and the

Chamber of Skulls

Mark Randolph Watters

Illustrated by
Ken "Blacktop" Gentle

Mark Randolph Watters

King's Way Press
3721 New Macland Rd.
Suite 200-141
Powder Springs, GA 30157
www.kwp-books.com

Illustrations Copyright © 2016 by Ken Gentle
www.blacktopfolkart.com

For *Kristyn*, my gorgeous; witty; and VERY smart daughter. She keeps alive my spirit of childhood and is the author of my inspiration.

For *Chris*, my devoted, loving wife and an incredibly hard-working, perseverant, and dedicated professional.

In recognition and celebration of our **30**th wedding anniversary, October 18, 2016.

**"What we do for *ourselves* dies with *us.*
What we do for *others* remains
immortal."**

--- Albert Pine

**"A friend may well be reckoned the masterpiece
of nature."**

--- Ralph Waldo Emerson

"So, Muley ... how was *your* weekend?"

--- Bobbi Leigh Harwell

Acknowledgements
and
Chamber Chat

It is with a skull's load (and that's a *lot!*) of appreciation that I acknowledge the following persons for their invaluable critique, suggestions, and feedback, all of which helped to make the *Chamber of Skulls* the coolest read in Raventon and in all the printed-word world!

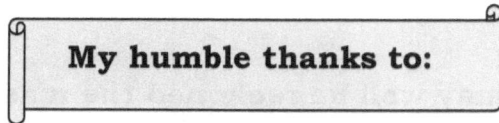

My humble thanks to:

Chris Watters – who picked the ticks (and how!) out of the text; **Kristyn Watters** – lovely daughter and reader extraordinaire; **Ken Gentle** – folk artist, illustrator, and an all-around swell guy; **Nelle Watters** – lifelong teacher, volunteer, and thumb of green; **Trina Watters Smith** – incredible oil-on-canvas artist and high-flyer; **Tracy Page** – dispenser of kind words and encouragement; **Emma** and **Kate Page** – tween sisters who both loved the book (so they said, and I believe 'em!).

The Chambers

Taylor Smart and the Chamber of Skulls

.

1

And Then There Were Two

"Gone are the pathways a child followed home; gone like the sand and the foam."
– Dan Fogelberg

They called her Muley. She preferred Mewels, as in a spelling like Jewels, for its more feminine connotation, assuming such could be inferred. But, after some playful haggling and a spirited twist of irony, Taylor relented. She didn't mind Muley, even Mules, so long as folks spoke it with respect. A nickname, she believed, embodied one's essence, one's character. She had earned it, after all.

Mike had dubbed her 'Muley' five years ago upon learning of his beloved daughter's stubborn triumph over her three-year struggle with leukemia, a fight her doctors privately believed could never rise to the hope of a cure. That is, until the moment-of-truth lab results revealed the cancer conquered, gone, traceless, as if it had never existed. Taylor's persistent refusal to give quarter to her doubts, foothold to her fears, earned her a do-over of precious life.

"Get the phone, please, Mewels!" Susan shouted from the upstairs bathroom as she dabbed droplets of perspiration from her brow. Susan had not relented.

"Getting it, Mom!" Taylor replied, lifting the receiver. "Hello?"

"Mrs. Smart, please," the voice asked.

"Just a minute. Who's calling, please?"

The voice did not respond.

"Just a minute," Taylor repeated compliantly, placing the receiver softly on the coffee table.

Taylor hurdled upstairs two steps at a time, sensing from the caller the urgency of the call.

"Mom, phone," Taylor puffed.

"Who is it?" Susan asked, waving the dryer over her damp hair. "Can you take a message?"

"He didn't say," Taylor shouted over the dryer's drone, catching her breath. "Sounded important, though."

"*He?* Is it Mike? We expected him three days ago, and-"

"Mom, Dad would have talked to me," Taylor interrupted, "and he wouldn't have called the land line, not the way you bounce around. Besides, I know Dad's voice, and it's not Dad."

"Okay," Susan said with reluctance, placing the hair dryer on the sink counter. "I'm coming."

Susan hustled downstairs, damp and dried hair flailing alternately the air and her shoulders.

Taylor followed, her hands holding at bay the bounce of her special necklace.

Susan put the call on speaker to free her hands for hair brushing.

"Hello?" Susan answered, pushing hair from her eyes.

"Mrs. Smart, this is Detective Simmons from the Raventon, Georgia Police Department. Is your husband home?"

"Raventon? No ... um, no, he's not." Susan glanced at Taylor and reached to disengage the speaker. Picking up the phone and cradling it between her shoulder and head while brushing her hair, she ambled toward the hall between the living room and kitchen. "I've been expecting him, but he's not home yet. Something, uh ... something wrong, Detective?"

Taylor flopped onto the couch and half listened to her mom's words. She ran her index finger back and forth along the edges of each of the three blades of her projectile point necklace, the very necklace Dad promised would bring her luck.

Taylor Smart and the Chamber of Skulls

Taylor's Dad made this necklace a few years ago from points she had found walking one crisp autumn Saturday morning through the rain-slopped bottomlands along the Sequoia River. Taylor recalled the day Dad drilled careful, surgically precise holes through the bases of the ancient, fragile points and slid a strip of dried buckskin through the holes, producing for his daughter a priceless memento of Native American art.

Friends considered Taylor a captive, tortured even, by her twentieth-century throwback parents. Such 'horrible' moments spent relaxing with weekend picnics in the country; endless visits to museums; lectures on values, freedom, and how the nation came to be; the gathering of handmade crafts collected along less-traveled trails. And bad jokes, each dismissed like candy wrappers.

These were the sorts of things that dominated Taylor's relationship with her parents, and, despite her friends' wary warnings, she loved every moment of it. She pitied her friends for their ignorance of life's simple pleasures in a world tormented by technology, texting, and malls.

Taylor watched her mom's mouth move but tuned out the sounds. She closed her eyes. Her mind drifted to other weekend afternoons.

Along with Mom and Dad, Taylor entered one of the intimate chambers of the Haydn Center for the Performing Arts, the room's size perhaps that of her living room. The magnificent hand-hewn stone hearth dominated the oak paneled walls and rose like a monument through the 14-foot ceiling. She sat.

Despite the fireplace fire crackling in the very heart of summer, its flames sending upward the swirl of sparks, hints of its comforting aroma of hardwood smoke finding her nostrils, and the frenzied dance of orange-yellow light thrown into the otherwise darkened room, Taylor noticed the conspicuous contrast of cool dryness and the absence of a sweat-soaked shirt. Ah, the miracle of air conditioning! That alone was worth the time. Besides, the chairs came equipped with headrests and rockers. These elements, along with the soothing notes of a stringed quartet, formed the perfect storm of snooze.

The four musicians entered, bowed, and settled into their wingback chairs, the arms of which were richly sculpted mahogany, each stylistically tipped on arms' ends with hand-carved, finger-worn, laughing skulls. The skulls' curved grins seemed, on the one hand, to dare the audience to maintain conscious attention, while on the other hand suggesting such was deathly futile. Taylor enjoyed the subtle joke.

The musicians stroked their bows across the strings a few times, like runners stretching before a race, and, with a pluck or two, began Debussy's String Quartet in G Minor, Opus 10. Taylor cherished her family's love of such summer weekends spent in the lulling embrace of chamber music played in the air-conditioned rooms of the Haydn Center for the Performing Arts. Taylor's friends thought her strange.

Mark Randolph Watters

Taylor squirmed within the cuddle of the cushioned couch as her mom conversed on the phone with Detective Simmons. She smiled, basking in her reliving of the musical conversation between violins and violas that spoke *only* to her. They didn't, of course. The notes flowing from the instruments spoke to anyone within earshot, anyone with the sensitivity to care about such.

Nonetheless, Taylor embraced the music played in the Haydn Center for the Performing Arts as one of her closest personal companions. Her love for the Haydn Center seemed to overshadow her attraction to all other summer venues, even swimming pools, Mike and Susan believed. Though the Haydn Center indeed held a special place for Taylor, she knew better. A fresh-water pool during a Middleboro summer was worth a thousand concerts.

Perhaps Taylor loved the music for the music's sake; perhaps it was the air conditioning she loved. Maybe both. Or perhaps the Haydn Center provided the only bona fide refuge for fleeing the monstrous Middleboro mosquitoes that rode waves of heat like roving gangs.

The conversation continued.

"Not sure, ma'am. We found your husband's truck parked along state route 42 yesterday morning." Simmons heard Susan's gasp and was quick to add, "We don't suspect foul play, Mrs. Smart, but we do have to check this out. We found his keys on the driver's side floorboard and his cell phone on the seat. Most recent call had been made to you, three days ago. That's when we're assuming he parked the truck here. We're hoping he hitched a ride home or to a place you might be able to tell us."

"Why would he have done that, Detective? Hitch a ride, that is."

"Found the truck pretty much in the boonies, ma'am."

"Boonies?" What's-"

"The sticks, ma'am. The country, several miles from town. The truck's hood was raised and the engine had been tampered with, a couple of hoses pulled, oil cap missing, that sort of thing. He might have had engine trouble, and, not being able to fix it himself, started walking to town."

"Are your people looking for him?" Susan asked frantically.

"Not sure where to look, ma'am, which is why I'm calling you. We know Mike's been in Raventon renovating the old Hatcher place. Has he mentioned to you places in town he likes to go or people he associates with when he's not working on the house?"

Susan thought for a moment. "No, Detective, he hasn't. In fact, all he talks about when he's home *is* the house, about what a challenge it is and how beautiful it is," Susan said, her voice tapering to a whisper.

"He's certainly worked miracles on that old place, Mrs. Smart. I'm sure this is nothing, ma'am, but if you do hear from him, could you give me a call, just to let me know he's okay? 555-6200. I would appreciate it."

"Yes. Certainly, Mr. Simmons. Thanks ... thank you for your call."

Taylor's mouth moved, but Susan did not hear her words. Susan lowered the receiver slowly onto its cradle as she stared at nothing, her thoughts racing.

"Mom ...?"

Days turned into weeks turned into months, and still no word from Mike. Officially classified as a missing person, no additional trace of Mike Smart was found outside the old Hatcher place. Then came the last day of July of the following year.

Detective Simmons called to tell Susan of their discovery, of the shallow hole found in the woods on Tucker's Mountain. Hikers discovered a depression containing Mike's favorite red and yellow flannel work shirt stained with the dried remnants of apple pie and splotches of crusty paint; a pair of brown steel-toed work boots; and his Movado wristwatch, all covered carelessly with leaves, branches, and a thin layer of soil.

Curiously – and this was the hopeful thing for Susan and Taylor – the conspicuous lack of human remains associated within or nearby the shallow hole, nor traces of blood on the personal items or inside the truck, baffled police. Still, they suspected the worst. They had no firm reason to suspect otherwise. The search expanded, but the trail ran cold, if indeed more trail existed. Clearly, authorities believed him dead, perhaps murdered, but they stopped short of declaring such, for now.

Susan and Taylor resigned themselves to accept the worst as they made preparations to carry on their lives in their renovated house, the old Hatcher house that Mike had prepared for them those many months.

Taylor dragged her tired, sore body to the porch and plopped onto its inviting steps. Two days had passed since the packing began, but it felt like two weeks. Slurping what remained of her lemonade, she took in hand her arrowhead necklace and caressed its buckskin strand. Susan supervised the final loading of furniture and boxes into the truck. Taylor watched, imagining the truck filled not with modern conveniences but instead with ancient treasures.

Taylor, once upon a time, had vowed over ice cream with her dad that she would someday become a world-famous archaeologist and uncover the greatest trove of Native American artifacts since the discovery of the Mississippian settlement at Cahokia, even crack Cahokia's long-locked codes. Impressed with his daughter's resolve and sense of direction, Mike gave Taylor these words, also over ice cream: **"The *path* is *half* the *math* to *knowing* where you're *going*."**

Taylor hadn't yet deciphered the full meaning of this bit of parental wisdom-in-rhyme, perhaps a code all its own, but she loved playing with the flow of the words, believing that one day the meaning would pounce upon her, Tigger-like, when she least expected it.

Taylor stopped. A sort of epiphanic pounce came over her as she realized for the first time the conspicuous dullness that dominated what once were razor sharp flint edges. Time, usage, erosion, whatever the forces in play, she vowed a similar dullness would never numb the memory of her Dad.

Taylor managed a smile, her thoughts careening from images of the Haydn Center for the Performing Arts, to laughing armrest skulls, to losing sneakers in bottomland quagmires, to her dad's tortuous telling of "candy-wrapper" jokes. Not even the thud of dropping boxes or bumping furniture offered distraction.

No doubt, Mike Smart told the worst jokes. Stories, too, but his knack for storytelling at least possessed the charm of originality. His jokes, on the other hand, possessed the irritation of cliché and the pain of repetition, like scratching an itch raw. While his jokes sparked an occasional sympathetic laugh, they mostly provided fodder for behind-his-back ridicule.

Ask anyone in Middleboro the most annoying teller of jokes, if the need arose to ask such a question, and the answer one received, accompanied by a raised don't-you-know eyebrow, was an emphatic **"Mike Smart!"** Jokes preceded him, a reputation like gusts of wind before a thunderstorm. He prefaced most conversations with jokes, a staunch belief clinging to his mind, as kudzu to a telephone pole, that folks expected and wanted such, followed by another joke, then another, upon which the hearing of such might render one irreparably numb.

Mike Smart was a well-respected, community-conscious man, in constant pursuit of the optimistic side of people and things. Humor served as his icebreaker. But, like a kid at a carnival, once he had hopped aboard the joke-telling carousel, stopping him was as futile as stuffing raindrops back into clouds. One just had to wait him out or think fast.

Folks loved Mike Smart but kept their distance when in a hurry, waving from across the street or dreaming up excuses to excuse themselves. Mike's blind spot, his bubble of innocence, was his insatiable optimism, and no one, especially Susan, felt the real need to burst it. Taylor had learned over time to tolerate her dad's incessancy, his one glaring flaw.

Now his bad jokes were gone. He was gone.

"Some luck!" Taylor muttered, as she slid the necklace around her neck.

A different life with different friends, even a secret or two, awaited Susan and Taylor in the river town called Raventon.

2

Raventon

"What lies behind us and what lies before us are of tiny matters compared to what lies within us."

— Emerson

Taylor cupped the projectile points in her hands, as if cradling crown jewels. She gazed trance-like, clusters of rocks; pines; and power lines fleeing past her passenger-side window, out of her life and into the forest of her memories. Reality cloaked itself in the foliage of deception.

"Mom, what do you think *really* happened to Dad?" Taylor asked, her thoughts meandering like the winding road before her.

Susan pretended not to hear the question as she focused on keeping the truck between the lines.

"Do you think he's still ... alive?"

No answer.

Taylor pressed.

"He wouldn't have ... *abandoned* us ... would he?"

That question rattled Susan's attention like the crash of cymbals upside the ear.

"Of *course* not!" Susan shouted, irritated that such a question was pondered, much less asked.

"Sorry!" Taylor whispered, cowering curled against the door.

Susan sighed, realizing that Taylor had asked the question meant not as an irritant but as part of the evolving process of losing one of the two most important individuals in her world.

"I'm sorry, sweetie; I didn't mean ..."

"I know, Mom. It's okay."

They tacked on another mile before the thump of a pothole shattered the awkward silence and probably a box of dishes as well, the telltale muffle heard of the familiar clatter of glass.

Susan gave Taylor a smile and changed the subject. "Straighten up so your seatbelt will work."

Taylor was in no mood for the proper posture that ensured a functioning seatbelt, but she sat straight anyway and resumed her examination of the necklace. The finely chipped points hung to a point between her sternum and stomach. Taylor wore the necklace every waking moment, even during baths, a constant reminder and source of hope that hope still existed. Taylor had given up on luck.

The truck groaned up the steep incline of a mountain road, the pitch of the whine changing to an intermittent grind with every awkward change of the transmission's gears, producing a sedative effect akin to the chamber music of the Haydn Center.

Dad had said these were not true 'arrowheads' but projectile points, spear points or knives, and that real arrowheads were much smaller, lighter, and better suited for aerodynamic flight on thin cane shafts. The necklace points, Dad had said, predated the bow and arrow by perhaps four thousand years and likely were used as knives or other simple tools of survival in a world far more complex than she and Dad could ever know.

That was fine for Taylor because it only deepened the mystery of how the makers of these meticulously crafted flint points lived and played; whom they might have loved or hated; what inspired them; what saddened them; where they roamed; what made them laugh; how they died; and all questions in between. This projectile point necklace served as her sole link to the unwritten history of early Americans whom forever would be known only to her mind's eye and to God. Taylor's imagination was piqued most by the mystery of the things history did not readily reveal.

"Raventon city limits," Susan announced.

"*Finally!*" Taylor said with a gust of breath, as if she'd just crossed the finish line of some race.

She recalled fondly the spring weekends when she, Mom, and Dad piled into the Odyssey for unhurried day trips to battlefields, ancient cemeteries, winding backroads scarcely traveled, or to surface-hunt for Native American artifacts—"left-behinds" as her Dad called them—in plowed, rain-washed bottomland.

Taylor especially missed those moments, those lazy day-long plods through mud-clodded fields. The discovery of a sun-drenched artifact produced shouts of "Over here!", but that wasn't the point. Finding nothing, even on days when her sneakers became hopelessly mired in the muck, became as joyous as filling their pockets with points and pottery pieces.

The inconvenience of frequent pullovers for the purpose of reading historical markers, another of Mike's incessant habits, ignited Taylor's sense of wonder, of how things came to happen in worlds far removed from her own. Raventon was such a world.

Now Taylor found herself surrounded by another history as she admired the long rows of nineteenth-century buildings flanking the broadest, perhaps the longest, downtown main street she had ever seen. Stately, proud buildings fronted with Doric columns and arched windows competed for the eye's attention with the streetwise, pitted brick facades nurturing spurts of small trees sprouting from cracked mortar. Banners on light posts greeted visitors with ***"Welcome to Raventon! We're Wise! We're Alive! We're 175!"***

Shadows of trees mingled with spears of sunlight sprawled across the unhurried townscape. Shoppers ambled into and from angled store fronts that reminded Taylor of downtown Middleboro, only bigger.

Topping a tree-guarded hill to their right sat a statuesque brick tower crested on four sides by Roman-numeraled clocks. Craning for a better view, Taylor held her spaniel-mix puppy, Stacy, close to her chest. She lowered the truck's window, but a truck in the opposite lane rolled forward, its imposing trailer blocking any view. Deep, heavy bongs of the clock's hourly peal echoed through the still air and gave Taylor a sudden sense of well-being, as if cloaked in her dad's hug in a room filled with chamber music.

Competing with the clock were the bells of churches playing the notes of familiar, old hymns, favorite hymns that once filled her Sundays. Taylor glanced at the radio clock, glowing with a turquoise '4:00', puny and laughable in contrast with the tower clock.

Susan watched for street signs as she slowly maneuvered the hulking truck through the hollows of hovering five-story buildings. Shadows stretched, soaking up sunlight and snatching vehicle after vehicle into their dark holds, like lemmings over the cliff. Drivers, anxious for the respite of home, honked impatient horns, but Susan paid them no mind.

Ahead loomed a landmark Mike had spoken of with fondness, the town's historically rich cemetery, its tilted, weathered headstones and sculpted mausoleums covering an immense terraced hillside pocked by the erosion of foot traffic, water, and time. Around the base of Cemetery Hill, a crystal blue brook curled her calm, westward arm, fishermen dotting the laps of her banks.

Seeing the street sign just in time, Susan yanked the wheel left into the turn lane. The truck's engine struggled to pull its heavy load up the narrow streets of several downtown slopes. Susan gave silent thanks for automatic transmissions.

Oak trees ignored sidewalks as thick roots curled upward and extended outward, like tentacles, bursting through concrete cracks of the trees' own making. Sidewalks were hardly obstacles for these hearty giants.

Taylor Smart's mule-like tenacity, much like that of a venerable oak tree, gave her strength unmoving in the face of adversity. She planted herself firmly into a thought, an idea, a resolution, and held firm her grip, all the while shoving aside opposition. She had learned this lesson the hard way and was not about to soften. Relationships with her friends were no different.

Loyalty reigned supreme with Taylor as the foundational ingredient of any genuine friendship. She gladly accepted anyone as her BFF, but with conditions. Woe befall any friend who cheated on tests or spoke ill behind Taylor's back or, worst of all, squealed an oath-held secret. These friends Taylor banished to the murky shadows of her permanent no-friend zone (FF – Former Friend).

Regaining her friendship, starting with the formidable matter of cracking through Taylor Smart's concrete of stubbornness, her Muleyness, became all but impossible for the banished, no matter how deeply ran the roots of the relationship. Those friendships back home were strengthened by the unbreakable alloy of trust and respect. She hoped to find the same in Raventon.

Excited as they pretended to be, Taylor and Susan Smart headed into Raventon and the ambiguity of their future without their best friend and anchor, husband and Dad, Mike Smart. Taylor, particularly, felt the numb of emptiness. Though she never admitted it when she took his presence for granted, gone abruptly was her shield against a world unforgiving. Gone was her advisor, her shoulder in climates of crushing uncertainty. Gone was her reassurance that good triumphs over evil.

Susan, indeed, refused to accept the likelihood that Mike was dead. Instead, she clung to the tattered word 'missing', the fuel that drove and sustained her. Their approaching anniversary strengthened her resolve to hang on to her threadbare hope, despite the odds.

Taylor tilted her head against the door padding and half-dozed to the drone of the truck's engine. Blackbirds crisscrossed sprawling limbs, as if furiously ferrying messages of the Smarts' arrival, the echoes of their caws giving dread to the urgency of their flight. She wondered if she ever again would know the bliss of afternoons filled with crackling fires and chamber music. Stacy slept curled in Taylor's lap.

Mark Randolph Watters

3

The Hatcher House

"I long, as does every human being, to be at home wherever I find myself."

- Maya Angelou

Tight clusters of amber-red maple and golden gingko leaves twisted in a gust of autumn air and splashed against the windshield, tumbling onto the truck's hood and scattering to the pavement. Feathery cirrus clouds tickled the breathless heights of a waning sapphire sky.

Plastic skeletons, hanging from porches and tree limbs, pitched randomly about on string tethers. Grinning straw-filled scarecrows and witches, embellished on their flanks by hay bales topped with mums and pumpkins, stood erect on green lawns. Scowling jack-o-lanterns guarded steps and doorways. Halloween spirit lurked, ready to pounce.

Susan Smart looked for street signs, landmarks, anything that gave assurance she and Taylor were nearing their new home. She slowed and maneuvered the cumbersome, green-paneled 26-foot truck toward the curb, finding space sufficient to pull forward and backward until the vehicle hugged closely to the curb, out of the way of the flow of traffic. She had rented a 16-footer, only to learn such was not available when she arrived to take the truck. The larger truck presented challenging, often troublesome, driving for Susan, but she had managed. Susan found strength in her resourcefulness.

Taylor Smart and the Chamber of Skulls

Bathed in shadow and light, clapboard houses loomed large down both sides of the autumn-colored street. The late afternoon sun peeked between the swaying branches of sprawling trees, many of which looked far older and more imposing than the houses they fronted. Taylor squinted.

Susan compared photos of their refurbished antebellum house to the real things dominating the oak-shrouded streetscape. Many of the houses in this amply wooded downtown neighborhood predated–and, by way of miracles, had survived– the ravages of the Civil War. All, save one, exhibited the work of renovation and meticulous upkeep.

Susan knew the address to be '1331 Shadowood Lane' but none of the houses displayed street numbers posted on their doors or columns or mailboxes or on such places as one might expect. Susan bobbed her head back and forth, from picture to porch, in search of the match.

After an anxious minute, she smiled and whispered, "There."

"Mom, are we here yet?" a bored Taylor asked in her whiniest tone, yawning and rubbing her eyes. Stacy stirred in Taylor's lap.

Susan stared.

"Mom?"

"Yes, I do believe this is it, right here."

Taylor turned, her view met by their three-story house towering atop a gentle rise that formed the front and side yards. Her sleepy eyes widened.

"Is that ... *Wow!* Mom, is that *ours?*" Taylor asked, expecting a more modest dwelling. "*This* is what Dad was working on all those weekends?"

Just as Taylor asked her questions, her tired eyes caught what appeared to be an opaque face, muted by the gray crosshatching of an attic window screen, staring blankly from the narrow space between the borders of a slightly opened curtain. Susan did not notice it.

"Mom, are you expecting someone?"

"What, Taylor?"

Taylor Smart and the Chamber of Skulls

Taylor looked again, but the image had vanished, if it ever existed in the first place. The scarlet curtain, now still and undisturbed, covered the entire window. Taylor rubbed her eyes, trying to clear the film of sleep and the hallucinations of dreams, and looked yet again.

"Never mind," she said. "It's nothing."

"It's all ours, sweetie," Susan answered, inattentive to Taylor's observation. "Every wavy window and courtly column, ours. A genuine work of art!"

"Arf!" Stacy barked, squirming.

The pair exited the truck and stopped at the base of the sloping front yard. They stared in silence, as if paying respects to a sacred memorial.

Gentle, familiar old-town sounds coursed through the trees. Squirrels darted from limb to limb. Blue jays shrieked. Katydids whined. Crows cawed their cornfield conversations. Rye grass of India green, manicured to a consistent 3-inch height, covered the roughly acre-sized lawn. Baskets of bursting yellow and purple mums hung at three-foot intervals along the length of the porch. Large pumpkins lined the edges of the porch steps, as if awaiting their fate. Towering oaks, their branches thick and twisted, perfect for hanging tire swings, flanked the house.

Scanning the property, Taylor, in fact, noticed a swing of dangling asymmetry, the ropes looped once around its hulky limb host, producing the salient visual imperfection of the entire yard. The swing swayed to the breeze in a rhythmic half-rotation, as if someone invisible were using it.

"Dad did *this*? He never mentioned it to *me*. I mean, I knew he was renovating a house ... but *this*?

"The renovations, yes. The upkeep, I don't know. Mike was never much of a yard man."

Taylor cherished her belief with peacock pride in thinking her Dad told her everything about everything, that secrets held no stature in their relationship. But the sheer scope of this one-man project came as a surprise to Taylor. At once, she felt a pinch of disappointment, as if Dad had withheld vital information.

"How old is it anyway?" Taylor asked as she reached to pluck an intrusive dandelion.

"It belonged to his great-great-great-grandparents. They built it themselves back in 1840-something, I think. Succeeding generations added to it, a room here, an extension there, until *voila!* Your Dad was getting ready to move us into this house when he … came missing." Susan paused. "He particularly wanted to surprise *you* with this house."

"Surprise *me?*" Taylor asked.

"He loved surprising you, Taylor. He told me six years ago–you were almost six when we reacquired this house that had once been in his family for generations–that he wanted to completely renovate it as a surprise for you. It was a mess then and needed lots of tender loving care. The owners had really let it go, much of the roof gone; boards bowed and glass broken; wood rotting; paint mildewed and peeling. Raventon, in fact, had condemned it. So, he bought it for a song and-"

"A song? What *song?*" Taylor asked, confused.

"Just an expression. Means he bought it cheaply, for taxes owed. Anyway, he refurbished the place, one weekend at a time. Rewired and replumbed it; installed modern conveniences. This is where your dad was during all those Saturdays, getting this place into shape, for us. He built a playhouse for you in the backyard and custom-designed your bedroom. This is where he wanted your best childhood memories-"

Susan lowered her head and cleared her throat.

Taylor wrapped her arms around Susan's waist. "We're going to be all right, Mom. I just *know* it."

"Isn't it *beautiful,* Taylor?" Susan managed with a whisper.

"It is, Mom," Taylor agreed, admiring the house's majestic, columned façade and throne-like porch spanning the breadth of its frontage. "Even Stacy likes it. Can we check out the inside?"

Stacy wagged her stubby cocker tail as her feathery black hair brushed the lush lawn.

Susan opened her mouth to answer, when from next door came a melodic shout.

Mark Randolph Watters

4

Miss Peasy

"To be yourself in a world that is constantly trying to make you something else is the greatest accomplishment."

- Emerson

"*Yoo-hoo!* Hey, there! Name's Miss Peasy," drawled the shrill, cracking voice of an elderly woman, stumbling, nearly falling, and deftly catching herself with the plant of her cane and the extension of her left arm, the hand of which held a Zippy burger.

Miss Peasy possessed an unquenchable need for stage center, as if the caricature of her cackling voice, like the sound of fingernails across a ripe chalkboard, did nothing to accomplish that on its own. She descended the front steps of her purple-painted, shadow-throwing Victorian-style house next door to the Smarts. A snow-white cockatoo stood with an impervious perch, like a marble statuette, upon her left shoulder.

"Miss Peasy Parlevous. And, no, I do *not* speak French, so you might as well *not* bother to ask! This here's Percival," she said, referring to the cockatoo.

Susan and Taylor exchanged quick, dumbstruck side glances. They did not ask.

"Um, hello, Miss ... Parlevous," Susan answered.

"Call me Miss *Peasy!* Short for Peasall. I was told my Daddy gave me that name; only God knows why. Anyway, addressing one by one's first name is as good as a handshake and a hug, *better* even, don't you think? Quickest way to a lasting friendship, I always say.

"My Daddy was a Parlevous, from New Orleans," Miss Peasy cackled, ambling down the slope of her yard with quick pecks of her cane upon the grass, her words echoing wall to wall, tree to tree, "though he spoke only two words of French himself, those being 'Merci beaucoup', as he shamelessly held a tin cup out for strangers to fill with their good luck. The depression beat down my daddy pretty hard, beat us all down. Me, I was never much for the name."

Miss Peasy stuffed the final bite of the Zippy burger into her mouth. She chewed with mouth wide open, oblivious to the disgusting sound of crinkling saliva, not to mention the visual horror, and swallowed, promptly refilling her mouth with a stick of some chocolate-colored substance pulled from her apron pocket. The Zippy burger wrapper rode a gust of air as it tumbled along the ground across the Smart's yard, lodging in the tangled hold of an azalea bush.

"You may call me Miss Peasy," she repeated; "it's *easy!*"

Miss Peasy giggled and chewed as she wriggled her threadbare garment through a gap in the line of waist-high boxwoods that separated the two yards, her hand-carved wooden cane probing and tapping each step of the way as if to give warning to any unseen object in her path.

"I'm such a little rhymer, don't you think?" Miss Peasy declared. "Peasy, easy." Her giggling increased as the satisfaction sank in. "Got another one. Wanna hear it? Well, you're going to." She cleared her throat. "Witches fly; Goblins cry; Souls moan; Creatures groan; Clouds tatter; Raindrops patter; Bats may bite; It's Halloween night! Well? What do you think? It's my Halloween muse."

Goes well with your 'whacky' muse, thought Taylor, irreverently.

Miss Peasy Parlevous brought one to mind of a drab, potato-stuffed burlap bag, alive and kicking. Her meandering gray hair, like the pricked and unwashed fibers of a well-worn

sweater, tussled untamed in the breeze. Each
strand of hair struggled to escape the grip of the
tilted, snug-fitting baseball cap covering Miss
Peasy's head, a strange cap indeed, grayish white
and emblazoned with the stitchings of two rows
each of five brown running stick figures, primitive
figures, like cave drawings.

The frizz of her hair, crowded by the cap,
held little comparison to the bush of her eyebrows,
two furry silver-gray caterpillars angled above her
eyes and barely separated by a crevice of
weathered skin.

Around her neck hung a leather necklace
strung with garlic bulbs, buckeyes, and dried
banana peppers. The only color to speak of on this
human tumbleweed gleamed from the emerald of
her eyes, a rich, glistening green such as one might
find on a glass frog in a souvenir shop.

"And it is *Miss*, mind you, not Mrs. I live
alone–have all my life–right here in Raventon.
Never known the assistance of a man, nor have I
needed such, as I have handled quite admirably

each and every home and auto repair the ineptitude of humans has thrown my way."

Miss Peasy gave a full brown-toothed smile, filled with the confidence of experience, each tooth flashing the distracting, unsavory sight of a mixture of saliva and the mysterious chocolate-colored substance.

Susan instinctively placed her palm over Taylor's gaping mouth and was tempted to do the same with her own had she not caught her mouth slipping wide and stopping it beforehand.

"Peased ... um ... *pleased* to meet you, Miss Parle–Miss Peasy," Susan said, clearing her throat and reflexively extending her hand in neighborliness. Taylor smiled uncomfortably as she shifted her weight from foot to foot, both hands behind her back.

"No worry, Mrs. Smart, no worry at all. Happens all the time. And I don't shake hands," she said, burying her ten crooked fingers under a fold of her apron. "No offense, but a body should pay careful heed to what bugs might lurk on hands and fingers, you understand, critters unseen like snakes in tall grass. I watched your husband put life back into this old house. Mmmm, pie's smellin' awful good, don't you agree?"

Miss Peasy bounced effortlessly from one topic to the next as she turned to spit a glob of the dark, slimy substance to the ground, a tad of the goo sliding down her angled chin. Wiping her chin with her forearm, she scanned the house side to side and top to bottom.

"Me, I'd never have done it," she declared. "No sirree, Bob. Though I *could* have, mind you. Best leave this spooky place *be*, I've always believed. But I do admire his craftsmanship. He had a way with the art of carpentry, with wood. Almost gooder'n me."

Taylor's ears perked at Miss Peasy's last remark. Zippy Burger wrappers tumbled across the breeze-swept yard.

"Miss Peasy, this is my daughter, Taylor."

"Nice to me–." Taylor stopped midsentence, staring at Miss Peasy's companion. "Is that bird *stuffed?*" Taylor blurted. "It looks ..."

"Such a *pretty* child!" Miss Peasy observed, pinching Taylor's words along with her cheek. Stacy gave a muted snarl from between Taylor's feet. "Looks a lot like her daddy, though don't get me wrong, Mrs. Smart, she favors you, too. Same eyes as you, blue as cornflowers, they are, but she has her daddy's black curls and cleft chin. Cuter'n a pig in warm mud, you are! Percival ain't stuffed, sweetie, but he *can* be a might stuffy! Takes some gettin' used to. Like me. Say, you strike me as pretty *smart*, just like your name says. Up for a riddle? Course you are! Ain't a 12-year-old girl alive what don't like riddles and boys, and, well, since I'm fresh out of boys ..."

Taylor issued a growl under her breath.

"Okay, here 'tis," Miss Peasy continued. "Why couldn't the sailors play cards?"

Taylor feigned puzzlement. Susan reached to calm Stacy's jitters.

"Give up?" Miss Peasy asked.

"Because the captain was standing on the deck," Taylor droned hurriedly.

"I knew it! I just *knew* you was a ringer! Now, could I interest you all in some apple pie and tea? Just pulled it from the oven. The pie, that is. *Haw!*"

'Almost gooder'n me'? thought Taylor, stunned by the crassness of Miss Peasy's braggadocios remark, not to mention her grammatical splintering of the phrase and the expulsion of that disgustingly slimy whatever-it-was. *This woman's flightier than a hot-air balloon!*

Miss Peasy's house, from the outside anyway, appeared ramshackle, shutters missing hinges; hinges missing shutters; paint peeling in wide, curling strips; window glass cracked, if not outright shattered; and scattered clusters of Zippy Burger wrappers and overturned drink cups.

If indeed Miss Peasy's carpentry skills were finer than Mike's, the evidence screamed otherwise. Besides, Taylor believed some things are better left unsaid, and Miss Peasy left *nothing* unsaid.

"No thank you, Miss-"

"No *need* to thank me, Mrs. Smart," Miss Peasy interrupted, arms and cane waving in the air as she turned toward her house and made her way between the boxwoods and up the slope of her yard. "I don't mind nary one bit sharing with my new neighbors. I'm only too happy to do it. Let me just get some forks and plates. Come now, mustn't dawdle! Just follow Percival!" she instructed as she flicked the bird off her shoulder. Percival squawked and flew a bowed path toward Miss Peasy's house and disappeared through a hole in the screened front door.

Susan and Taylor looked at each other and, with a gasp of awe and a shrug of surrender, followed Miss Peasy to her expansive front porch steps, which were covered with wood shavings, scattered nails, chunks of drywall, several buckets of half-used paint, and a slew of Zippy Burger wrappers. Maybe she had started some renovations of her own.

A few paces behind, the Smarts followed Miss Peasy, who, despite her advanced age, demonstrated fluency with navigating the switchback route carved amid the obvious peril of the debris-covered steps.

A group of crisp, white wicker chairs plush with magnolia-patterned downy cushions, upon which the Smarts picked two and sat, lined the porch.

The drive had been long, after all, and the two had not eaten since morning. A sweet snack and a moment's rest dangled as attractive lures, despite the utter peculiarities of Miss Peasy. The moving company would arrive soon anyway, meaning several hours more before the Smarts' enjoyment of any real rest. Might as well take advantage of some Peasy hospitality.

"Can't stay but a minute, Miss Peasy," Susan announced, wanting to give pre-emptive notice and a firm non-commitment. "Moving men'll be here soon, and–"

"All the more reason to sit a spell, take a load off your puppies and eat a bite," Miss Peasy said, smacking her palm on Susan's knee. "Why, I believe you've been on the road the better part of five hours, am I right? Long drive from Middleboro, what with all that construction through Sandville and the narrow two-lane mountain roads heading east and south. Nice waterfalls up yonder but no good place to view 'em 'less you're a passenger. Lordy! You drove that big truck over them mountain roads! Sit! *Sit!*" Miss Peasy demanded, pointing, even though Susan and Taylor had already sat.

Miss Peasy left and returned, quicker than her eighty-nine years suggested possible, and handed each a plate holding a triangular cut of apple pie, wedges of juicy, cinnamon-laden apples oozing on crusty slides down the packed sides of each slice. Taylor thought of, and in the same instance dismissed, Miss Peasy's chin and the gooey, dark stuff. The pie's warm aroma wafted gloriously, hauntingly hypnotic and sedating, its rising steam seeming to curl knowingly into her nose.

"Go on, now, *eat up!*"

"Thank–thank you, Miss Peasy," Susan said as she slid her fork under crust.

Miss Peasy stood over the two, eyes widened, lips pursed, breath bated, and hands wrung, as if she were awaiting the announcement of the county fair's blue ribbon winner.

"I do hope you find it satisfying!" Miss Peasy said, unable to remain silent. "The recipe has been passed down since before the Revolution. Still have the original paper it's written on, though it's now under airtight glass, you see."

Miss Peasy gave a wink and pulled a pipe and a pouch of cherrywood tobacco from the pocket of her apron.

"I never partake inside a house, mind you, but the embrace of a cushioned wicker on one's own front porch in the middle of a quiet evening ...

is quite the perfect place and time, don't you think, Mrs. Smart?" Miss Peasy sat.

"Y-yes ... quite," Susan replied with surprise. "If one smokes, that is, which I–"

"See, I got me this pain, right here in my hip," Miss Peasy explained as she tilted right and patted her left side. "Doc Hollister's been giving me pills going on thirty years, and they relieved the pain quite well. Until about this time last year, anyway. That's when the pills stopped working. Just stopped, they did. I didn't know what I was going to do about my pain.

"But then I began to notice the soothing aroma of cherrywood tobacco smoke, Doc Hollister's favorite blend. One can't really help *but* notice it, even when it ain't burning. Have you met the good doctor, Mrs. Smart?"

"Can't say that I have, Miss Peasy, what with our just arriving."

"True, true. You wouldn't have had the time. Salt of the earth, Doc Hollister. Cute as a bug-eyed turtle!" Miss Peasy said through a rising grin.

"I think he's sweet on me, except he's a might younger, being seventy-four. Keeps me spry, though!

"Anyway, that's also when I noticed the pain fading in my hip. Two and two, you know. And since I don't believe much in *coinkidinks!*"

Miss Peasy smiled, tapping the upturned bowl of her pipe against her hip, powdery ashes swirling into the air.

Taylor whispered out of the side of her mouth, "Mom, what's a *coinkidink?*"

Miss Peasy continued, unaware of Taylor's query.

"So I got myself down to Liberty Tobacco on Main Street, picked me out this cute Winslow briarwood pipe, and here I am! Hip's fit as an October barn dance, too!

"Too bad you don't enjoy a pipe now and again, Mrs. Smart. It's not exactly smoking, technically that is, not like cigars and the like, such nasty pieces of filth, they are! It's more like *puffing*, if you get my meaning.

"I know it ain't ladylike," Miss Peasy admitted apologetically as she pinched some tobacco from the pouch and stuffed it into the pipe's bowl, "and it's certainly not the example to set before a child, I reckon, but then it *is* aromatic and relaxing. Liberating, too, sort of like rewarding yourself for a job well done, and, well, I ain't *got* me no children to be settin' examples before, so ..." Miss Peasy cackled.

"Why not just pick yourself some flowers?" Taylor blurted. "*They're* aromatic-"

"Um ... pie's *delicious*, Miss Peasy," Susan inserted, nudging Taylor with her foot, "simply delicious."

"Why, thank you, Mrs. Smart! Thank you, indeed! I just *love* your daughter's black curls!"

Scratching a match across the bottom of her shoe, Miss Peasy winked at Taylor and lit the tobacco, puffing rapidly to give the flame life, releasing the cherrywood aroma.

Taylor and Susan shuffled uncomfortably in their chairs, twinges of pain shooting through *their* hips.

"Yes. Yes, the pie's wonderful, Miss Peasy," Taylor agreed. "Well, Mom, the moving men will be here shortly. Guess ... um ... we should go prepare to receive them?"

"Guess so, Taylor."

"Leaving so soon?" Miss Peasy asked, the pungent smell of cherrywood smoke filling the crisp air and overwhelming the apple pie.

"It's been quite a day, and it's far from over. We do appreciate your kindness, Miss Peasy. Perchance I might have your recipe?"

"For my kindness or for the pie ... perchance?" Miss Peasy replied, rewarding her self-perceived wit with a hearty laugh and drawing another puff from her pipe.

Susan shared a contrived laugh.

"I'd love to give you my apple pie recipe, Mrs. Smart, really I would ... but I won't. Can't. Family secrets should remain such, don't you agree? Good evening to you both."

And with that, Miss Peasy pulled the squeaky screen door shut behind her and vanished into the darkened recesses of her way-too-big-for-one-solitary-old-lady home.

"Well," Susan said after a cricket-interrupted pause to see what other surprises might spring forth from Miss Peasy Parlevous, "shall we be going?"

Both glanced around a bit uneasily for a spot to set their plates and forks, finally opting for the seats of the wicker chairs.

"She's coming back out, Mom," Taylor predicted. "To get the plates."

"No, I don't think so, Taylor."

They paused for an extra few seconds, just to be sure, staring at the silent screen door.

Satisfied, Susan said, "Okay, let's get ho–"

"So, who's going *flying* with me?" Miss Peasy asked, her frizzed, capped head poking out the door like some frazzled bird of a cuckoo clock.

5

Up for It?

"Flying is learning how to throw yourself at the ground ... and miss. "

-- Douglas Adams

"Um, did you ... did you say *'flying'*, as in an *airplane?*" Taylor asked, with a tilt of a disbelieving grin and the arch of one eyebrow. Not that Taylor did not *want* to fly; she *did*. Just not with Miss Peasy.

"That I did, young lady! Ain't *no* other way, if it's a good time you're looking for! Up for it?"

Miss Peasy stepped out onto the porch, her thumbs curled around the shoulder straps of her apron, chin up, as if she'd just announced her candidacy for public office.

"Miss Peasy, I don't think-"

"Now, *calm* yourself, Mrs. Smart. I know what you're thinking, and if I were you, I'd be thinking the same thing, maybe *worse*."

"You're a *pilot?*" Taylor asked.

"Going on sixty-nine years, Miss Taylor. Own my own plane, too, a Cessna Skyhawk four-seater! Like I said, you up for it?"

Susan offered a dismissive chuckle. "Miss Peasy, thank you, but if you're talking about taking Taylor for-"

"Cool! Mom, can I *go?*" Taylor said with a sudden reversal of heart, excited at the prospect of expanding her horizon way beyond her five-foot-high point of view. Or maybe she just enjoyed watching her mom squirm.

"Taylor, I don't think-"

"Then it's *settled!*" Miss Peasy said with a clap of her hands. "Let me just go turn off the oven – pie, you know – and, Mrs. Smart, if you'll be so kind as to drive us to the airport. I don't drive anymore, you see. Haven't for fifteen years. So, I'll just go turn down the fire and lock the door. Plane's all gassed up."

"*Wait* a minute!" shouted Susan. "Just a darn minute here!"

Miss Peasy leaned toward Taylor and whispered, "I think I've gone and made your mom mad."

Taylor smiled.

"You *fly* a plane but you don't *drive* a car?" Susan asked, irritated more by her inability to process the sheer unpredictability of one Miss Peasy Parlevous.

"Guilty as charged, Mrs. Smart! There was a time when I saw the need, but I gave it up to all the nuts on the road." Miss Peasy then pointed upward. "Ain't nobody crossing the center line up yonder or runnin' red lights while texting on their cell phones. Besides, flying's funner!"

"*Funner?* Miss Peasy, you are *not* taking my daughter for a ride today, or *any* day, in any airplane, end of story!"

"Aw, *Mom!*"

"Enough, young lady. We appreciate your delicious pie, really we do, but we've got moving and unpacking to finish," Susan said tactfully and with strained restraint for her genuine feelings.

"Then I reckon tomorrow would be a better time?" Miss Peasy asked.

"Mom, ask her about a *pilot's license*," Taylor advised.

Susan gave Taylor a stare of frustration tempered with disbelief.

"Got it right here, Mrs. Smart," Miss Peasy said, removing her cap and pulling a laminated document the size of a credit card from a pocket sewn within. She handed it to Susan, who took the card and, after puffing a frizz or two of hair off the card, read.

"Department of Transportation ...," Susan muttered, searing a visual path over the document.

"And the Federal *Aviation* Administration!" Taylor said, excitedly. "Not only that, but it says here '...has been found to be *properly qualified* ... private *pilot* ... date of issue June 2007.' Wow, Mom. She *is* a pilot!"

"That's just the renewal date," Miss Peasy clarified.

"Miss Peasy, I must confess my surprise. I mean, you're ... you're ..."

"An old woman?" Miss Peasy said, finishing Susan's obvious point.

"Well ... I didn't mean ... that is ..."

"It's okay, Mrs. Smart. I get this reaction all the time."

"How do I know this license is genuine and not ..."

"... and not some Cracker Jack surprise? Ain't but one way to find out, right?"

"So, they let you fly, by yourself?"

"By myself, day or night, rain or shine, like it or not. As long as I have a current license and medical clearance. To me, age and time are just numbers, concepts concocted by men so they'd have a convenient excuse for missing meetings, anniversaries, and church. I *do* have to prove myself worthy every six months, of course, but, yes, they let me fly." Miss Peasy spoke these words with pride, fully confident in her abilities, despite the real limitations of age, or those perceived.

"Flew two days ago, as a matter of fact. Ask Percival; he's my mascot and goes wherever I go. Appropriate, don't you think, the bird being a natural flyer. Wait right here. I want to show you something else."

Miss Peasy again disappeared behind her screen door, Percival firmly fixed upon her shoulder. Before Taylor could utter once more the question she hoped would affirm permission, Miss Peasy pushed open the screen door, which replied with a tortuous squeal of its hinges.

"Here," Miss Peasy said, flipping pages. "This is my flight log. See that entry?"

Miss Peasy handed the log to Taylor, who read, "October 27, 2010. Origination: Raventon, GA. Destination: Asheville, NC. Duration: Five hours, thirty minutes. Weather: blah, blah. Notes: blah, blah. This was just a couple days ago!"

Susan looked at Taylor, both silent. Taylor's eyes widened, aware that each second that passed in silence equaled a rising chance her mom would allow what seemed only moments ago the purest of folly.

"Miss Peasy, please understand that I am *not* onboard with this idea, not yet anyway. But, *if* - mind you, a *big* if - you can demonstrate to us that indeed you *are* a pilot *and* an owner of your own airplane, well, then ... I'll reconsider, *possibly*."

A drop of brown slime slid from Miss Peasy's smile, down her chin, and plopped to a porch plank. Percival bent forward, watching the drop's fall. Susan feigned a distracted focus on anything but the sight before her.

"I understand, Mrs. Smart, and that's all an old woman can expect."

Taylor flashed her broadest of smiles, sucking in a lungs-full of Raventon air, crisp, invigorating, exciting. *Miss Peasy may be kooky,* thought Taylor, *but she's **my** kind of kook!*

6

Ghost Ship

"Spooky is as spooky does."

- with apologies to Forrest Gump

"I'll call on you in the morning, Taylor," Miss Peasy said.

"Better make it the afternoon, Miss Peasy," Susan said, "say around four-ish? We've got a ton of work to do before we can play. Even then, Sunday might be best."

"Sunday it is, then. How does 1:00 sound?"

"Sounds *great!*" Taylor shouted. "Thank you, Miss Peasy!"

"You're as welcome as bees in honeysuckle!"
Miss Peasy answered.

Miss Peasy melted into the depths of her
home, her head swimming with the energy of
renewal and possibilities.

Taylor and Susan returned to their new
home, speaking often of Miss Peasy, both of whom
agreed, despite her obvious friendliness and
unusual skills, warranted some careful watching.

Original planks of hardwood spit out
mournful creaks with nearly every step on their
tour of the house, rendering conversation about
most anything a waste of effort.

"Won't be able to sneak out of *this* house,"
Taylor observed with the slanted resign of a smile.

Ceilings, fourteen feet high, gave each room
its own enormity and each occupant a sense of
ample space. Taylor, once fearful her dormant
claustrophobic tendencies might re-awaken in a
different house, thought nothing of it.

Blackened fireplaces spoke of generations
when, besides peaks of sun through tall, curtained

windows, such were the only sources of light and warmth and were witness to snug family conversations and blankets of storytelling.

Crystal chandeliers, their glints of reflected light casting a meandering of prism rainbows on the walls, hung and glistened like clusters of icicles. Ancient cobwebs curved from crystal to crystal.

Narrow ceiling-to-floor windows allowed the fleeting entry of afternoon sunlight and cast eerie shadows that angled along the walls like sharp, clutching fingers.

An odor of age, ancient and enveloping, clung to every surface and found unrelenting passage into every nostril.

"It's gorgeous, Mom, but we've got to take care of that smell," Taylor said, waving her hand over her nose.

"We'll just throw open the windows, air the place out. Some incense will help, too."

"Potpourri," Taylor replied. "Maybe gardenias."

"Maybe."

"Mom, are you serious about maybe letting me go up in an airplane with Miss Peasy?"

"What I'm serious about is knowing without *any* shadow of a doubt that she is competent and safe. Her plane, too."

"So, if all that checks out on Sunday, I get to go up?"

"*We* get to go up. Don't forget, I have my pilot's license, too. I'm not ready to turn over my only daughter to anyone's care, competent or no. But only if the plane checks out. Anyway, an extra pilot never hurts, especially in this case."

"Oh, Mom, you're just like ... Dad."

Taylor's eyes locked onto Susan's. They shared a hug.

"This is odd," Susan observed upon climbing the attic stairs.

"What, Mom?"

"In that corner."

Susan pointed to the word '**BOO!**' scribbled awkwardly in black paint on the white wall.

"Would *Dad* have done that, Mom?"

"Seems unlikely. It's not like him to deface such a smooth, skillful paint job, unless he has some concept in mind, maybe something like a Halloween Room, for you. He never mentioned doing anything of the sort, but you know your Dad."

"Over here, Mom!" Taylor shouted.

Susan rushed to another attic room, to Taylor's voice. Taylor pointed to the crudely painted image of a horned, pitch-forked devil, under which were the words, '**Got You!**'

"Dad did *this?* Not sure I like the Halloween Room idea."

"No, Taylor, your father would never have painted this." Susan drifted from attic room to attic room, giving each a quick inspection. "I wonder if Detective Simmons and Sheriff Hagan are aware of this."

"Could be a vandal's doing, Mom," Taylor suggested.

"Could be, Taylor, and likely is, but nothing's broken or stolen. Downstairs is pristine, full of fixtures any vandal or thief would sink their claws into."

Directly a knock came upon the front door.

"Moving men, Mom!" Taylor shouted, peering out the window to the street below.

The movers worked mechanically, silently, into the darkness, unloading dozens of pieces of furniture; a baby grand piano; appliances; and scores of half-sealed, misshapen boxes filled with dishes, clothes, and books.

Susan and Taylor, meanwhile, performed the important work of assembling the beds and placing the mattresses and box springs.

Finishing half past midnight, the movers accepted their pay, plus a handsome tip and bottles of cold spring water. They thanked Susan for her business, and made their exit.

Susan sighed as the movers drove away. She pushed shut the massive mahogany front door, resting her weary body against its paneled relief. A ringing silence rushed into her ears.

"Not doing *this* again!" Susan announced without much surprise. "Boil some water, Taylor, please."

Exhausted to the point sleep was impossible, Susan plopped onto the sofa. Stacy napped blissfully by the brick fireplace.

Friday nights held promise for the relaxation of Mom-daughter restaurant dates, a special time to unwind and reflect, but bites here and there on peanut butter sandwiches sufficed this night. Their car had not yet been delivered, and Susan was in no mood to drive a 26-foot moving truck on a midnight food hunt. Neither knew Raventon well enough to venture out past dark. Besides, thunder rolled in the distance like a lullaby.

"Water's boiling!" Taylor announced.

"Can you make me a cup of tea? A touch of honey and dab of milk. Thanks!"

"A touch and a dab, just the way you like it. I'm on it." Taylor poured some milk for herself. "Mom?"

"Mmm, hmmm."

"Are you still a writer?"

"Still a writer, sweetie," Susan answered, resting the back of her hand on her forehead, eyes closed. "Why do you ask?"

"I dunno. Just wondering how we're going to survive in this huge house and tiny town, that's all. Here's your tea, touched and dabbed. Careful."

"Thank you so much, sweetheart. My clients aren't here in Raventon. They're all over the country, New York, Chicago, LA, Peoria. You just worry about school, young lady, which reminds me. We need to find out where your new school is." Susan slurped her hot tea and sighed. "Tomorrow."

"Tomorrow's Saturday, Mom. Can't it wait until Sunday?"

Taylor Smart and the Chamber of Skulls

The two sat silently, one with eyes closed and the other marveling at the ceiling height, each processing the events of the day, and one Miss Peasy, in her own way. The sound of thunder crept closer as lightning pierced curtainless windows and the black veil of the dead of night.

"That Miss Peasy is sure a strange one, Mom."

"Is that such a nice thing to say about our thoughtful, new neighbor? The pie was wonderful, and she didn't *have* to offer it."

"Thoughtful maybe, and yes, the pie was super, but smoking a pipe?"

"I admit that's rather strange behavior all right, for an old woman, anyway."

"For *any* woman! And that stuff she spit!" Taylor added. "What *was* that? Gross!"

"Don't ask," Susan replied, touching her lips with three fingers, as if to hold back a retch. "She's quite the eclectic."

"Mom, do you think she's really a pilot, owns her own plane and all?"

"I don't know why she would lie about a thing like that, sweetie."

"I suppose so," Taylor agreed, though still unconvinced as to Miss Peasy's authenticity.

Taylor had observed before how some grown-ups tend to overstate accomplishments, if not outright lie about them. Perhaps this was one of those times.

"I think she's too aggressive," Taylor observed, "brags too much. Just plain *talks* too much, if you ask me, slinging herself from one thing to another like a pinball.

"And that house! Looks like she's tearing it *down*, not fixing it up! I missed stepping on a nail by *this much!*"

Taylor parted her index finger and thumb a half inch or so to illustrate how close she'd come to a doctor's visit and tetanus shot. Though quite experienced with such, Taylor hated needles and didn't desire them thrust upon her again, especially by the negligence of others.

"I admit her house *was* a mess on the outside," Susan replied, "and that she talks like a blue jay. But maybe she's earned the right to brag. What matters is that she has a clean heart."

"And a *pigsty* porch!"

"Sounds as if you're having second thoughts about this plane ride she's offered you. I've had third, fourth, and fifth thoughts, and counting! Even if everything checks out, Taylor, you do not have to fly with her. Miss Peasy has a lot more to prove than her wonderful apple pies before I'll allow you inside her airplane."

Taylor stared at the ceiling. "Anyway, Mom, I saw a face in our attic window, right after we arrived."

"*What?* You saw a *face?* In our attic window?" Susan immediately associated Taylor's statement with the words scratched on the attic room walls.

"Probably just shadows, but it sure *looked* like a face. Good grief, Mom! Did you hear *that?*" Taylor said, sitting erect and looking at the ceiling.

Stacy lifted her ears and eyes but kept her head rested on her paws.

"Storm's coming," Susan said.

"I'm not talking about the thunder, Mom."

CR-R-R-E-E-E-A-K-K!! CR-R-R-E-E-E-E-A-K-K!!

The sound bounced across the room with the dead rhythm of hardwood planks on an ancient ghost ship, rocking side to side on the ocean waves.

"That!"

Susan sat straight and looked up, trying to determine which second-floor room they were under. She listened.

"Taylor ... someone's up there!" Susan whispered, standing. "Where's my phone?"

"Mom, wait," said Taylor. "You left your phone on that shelf in the attic, remember?"

Both paused in silence for an agonizing minute, their communication lifeline well beyond reach.

"I don't hear anything now."

Outside, the approaching storm's rising wind swished tree branches and pushed against the house like omnipotent hands. Inside, the staccato ticking of the grandfather clock lulled the two into a trance-like state.

Then, the sudden, simultaneous explosion of lightning and thunder sent Susan and Taylor screaming face first into the sofa. Stacy rolled onto her side and sighed. Both laughed and briefly forgot the spooky sounds heard above them only moments before.

Mark Randolph Watters

7

Bobbi Leigh Harwell

"A friend may well be reckoned the masterpiece
of nature."

- Emerson

Knock! Knock! Knock!

Taylor looked at her mom. "Are you expecting someone, Mom?"

"At 1:30 in the morning? I don't think so! This is getting *too* weird." Susan injected a bit of Halloween humor into an increasingly strange scenario. "Only the ... *dead* ... are out *this* time of night! *Wa, Ha, Ha!*"

"The *dead?* Mom! Maybe it's just the wind blowing the mum baskets around or something," Taylor suggested as she made a ball of herself in a corner of the sofa.

Knock! Knock! Knock!

"In *triplicate?* Those aren't the mums. I better check this out, Taylor. You stay put," Susan instructed with a firm shaking of her finger as she grabbed one of Taylor's baseball bats.

Susan moved slowly toward the front door, bat cocked ready for whatever pitch was coming. Lightning exploded through the windows casting eerie, split-second flashes of light and shadows on the walls. Thunder responded.

Susan leaned and rested her right ear against the door.

"Who's there?"

No answer.

"Who's *there?*" she repeated.

"It's *me!* Bobbi *Leigh!* Your neighbor down the road!"

"Our neigh-," Susan mumbled in frustrated surprise, unlocking the deadbolt.

"Hi," said Bobbi Leigh, her face planted against the screen door, the contortion giving Susan a startle. "I'm Bobbi Leigh Harwell, your neighbor down-"

"Yes, you *said* that. Come in out of that weather, Bobbi Leigh."

The wind pushed fallen leaves across the porch, through the opened door and into the foyer. Bobbi Leigh swept the red mid-back-length strings of hair from her face.

"Getting stormy out there," she said, wiping her shoes on the floor mat.

"No kidding," Susan acknowledged as she gazed curiously at Bobbi Leigh. "Not to mention *late.* Taylor, we have a … visitor. Bobbi Leigh, my daughter, Taylor. Taylor, Bobbi Leigh. And this little guy is our cocker spaniel, Stacy."

The girls exchanged nods.

"You said three prepositions in a row, Mom."

"What? Three ... *what?*"

"Prepositions. 'Come *in* ... *out* ... *of* ... that weather.' Three prepositions in a row."

Susan had no reply for Taylor, except jaw-drop.

"Beautiful dog!" observed Bobbi Leigh, quickly changing the subject. "I just *love* black dogs, especially cockers and labs with patches of white on their chests. So *cute!* My lab, Champ, is the same color, only much bigger, of course."

"Well, being a lab-" Taylor countered. "How come they call you Bobbi Leigh?"

Susan interrupted, "Taylor, 'in' and 'out' were used as adverbs, not prepositions."

"What are you people *talking* about?" Bobbi Leigh asked.

"Um, Bobbi Leigh, speaking of '*out* there', I have to ask you ... what are *you* doing *out there* at *1:30* in the morning? And with a storm coming, no less. Do your parents know?"

"Out of town, both of them," Bobbi Leigh replied with a shrug. "But they probably know anyway. I do this all the time. Anyway, I couldn't sleep, and Ifs got spooked by the thunder, so I decided to take him for a walk while it wasn't raining. Ands and Buts, too."

"Ifs, Ands ... and Buts? They your dogs, too?" queried Taylor.

"Yep, two German shepherds and an Irish setter. Buts is the setter." Bobbi Leigh smiled. "They're out there sniffin' a pile of leaves. They could probably use the bathroom break, too. All three can find just about anything, anywhere. When they get the scent, say a raccoon's, they'll track it forever until they find it. My dogs are how I came to get baptized."

"*Baptized?*" Taylor blurted. "Your dogs *baptized* you?"

"No, silly! I was out playing with the dogs one Sunday morning–weren't nobody home but me–and, well, it came up a cloud, raindrops falling harder'n a bag of marbles! Seems to do a lot of that in Raventon, rain, that is.

"Anyway, I was just a seed-spit away from the church. So, I ran inside; dogs, too. I stayed dry while them marbles fell, and I listened to the preacher. A few weeks later, I got myself baptized, a full-body dunk in Frog Bottom Creek. Guess you could say I come in out of the rain and ended up all *wet* despite it all!"

"There are those three prepositions again," Taylor said with frustration.

"*Adverbs* and prepositions," Susan whispered. "Interesting names for your dogs, Bobbi Leigh."

"Funny how they got those names, too! I begged my Dad for a puppy two years ago. He said what all parents say, 'Maybe someday' and 'We'll see', you know, things parents say when what they really mean is 'no' but can't bring themselves to say 'no'."

Susan cleared her throat and managed a grin.

"Anyway, Dad soon got tired of my begging, and after I grabbed some stray dog and brought it home, he hit the roof. Dad did, not the stray dog. I still remember his exact words: 'What if he had *rabies*! Just because he doesn't have a collar doesn't mean nobody owns him! You're not getting *any* dog, Bobbi Leigh, not after what you've pulled! Don't ask me again! No dog for you! No ifs, ands, or buts about it.' Well, the rest, as they say, is history."

Bobbi Leigh gave a toothy smile, the sort of smile a kid smiles after sweet, total victory.

"Your parents are out of town, and you're home alone?" Susan asked.

"That's about the size of it, Mrs. Smart. It's okay. They do *that* all the time. Careers, you know."

"How do you know-"

"*Everybody* knows who y'all are," Bobbi Leigh said, smacking her chewing gum and craning her neck for views of the massive rooms. "We've known you were coming ever since Mr. Smart began fixing up this place. Too bad they never found-"

Bobbi Leigh caught herself and instead turned her attention to the living room. Lightning flashed brighter and thunder rolled louder.

Susan glanced at Taylor.

"So, Taylor," Bobbi Leigh blurted between gum smacks, "wanna be friends? I'm twelve years old and in the 7th grade, same as you, I reckon. I'm one of your classmates at Raventon Middle School. You'll love our teacher, Mrs. Hanson. I'll show you around on Monday and give you a heads-up on all the weird stuff. You know, who and what to avoid, stuff like that. Word of advice: *bring* your lunches! Plus, I could use your help with those preposition and adverb things!"

"Friends? Well ... sure, I guess-"

"Great! And they call me Bobbi Leigh 'cause that's what they *named* me! *Duh!* Dad says it's a Southern thing. Call me Leigh if it makes you feel better, but the world's *full* of famous girls named

Bobbi. Let's see, there's Bobbi Gentry; Bobbi Jo
Bradley ..."

Bobbi Leigh stopped, but her fingers kept
counting.

"I don't know who all; a *bunch* of 'em,
though! Well, I just wanted to stop by, say hello,
be neighborly and junk. Guess I better go find the
dogs before the rain sets in. Could be just a
lightning storm," she said casually as if *that*
weren't dangerous enough. "They're probably
hiding in a ditch, chewing on squirrels. Hey,
Taylor, I know this great cave down by Lake
Jasper. Maybe you an' me can go check it out
tomorrow ... I mean, *today!*"

"I don't know about the idea of going into a
cave, Bobbi Leigh," Susan said, intercepting the
idea before it took hold in Taylor's mind. "Anyway,
sleep first, and lots of it, then getting this house in
shape."

"Parents," Bobbi Leigh said with a shrug as
she hopped like a pogo stick down the porch steps.

"They're all alike, right, Taylor? See y'all tomorrow. No offense, Mrs. Smart!"

Taylor pondered the parents-are-all-alike comment. Maybe Bobbi Leigh was on to something.

Susan gushed with speechless surprise, not quite knowing what to make of Taylor's abrupt new friend. Thus far, the Smarts had met only two of Raventon's residents, and though the town might have appeared sleepy and boring, the same could not be said of the random sampling of its citizens.

"You mean *today*," Taylor whispered, rubbing her tired eyes and turning toward the stairway to her bedroom.

Susan locked the front door and watched out the window until Bobbi Leigh's silhouette disappeared from the glow of the porch light and into the strobe of lightning flashes.

Clutching the banister rail as if she were a hundred years old, Taylor climbed the wide staircase. She plopped onto her canopy bed and was asleep almost as soon as her head touched the stack of pillows. Stacy jumped onto the bed and curled around the top of Taylor's head.

Several minutes passed, just long enough to send Taylor into a deep sleep. Stacy, ever protective, lifted her head and perked her floppy ears at the sound.

CR-R-R-E-E-E-A-K-K!! CR-R-R-E-E-E-E-A-K-K!!

She whimpered slightly, shifted her back legs, and rested her head atop Taylor's.

Mark Randolph Watters

8

The Legend

"Every legend, moreover, contains its residuum of truth ..."

– James Baldwin

"Had a strange dream last night, Mom," Taylor said as she carved her syrup-soaked pancakes into neat rectangles.

"Tell me," Susan replied, her sleepless head resting in the palm of her hand.

"Well, I dreamt I was walking down a dark path, late at night, when suddenly I heard squeaky footsteps behind me, getting closer and closer. The steps were slow, like this–*E-E-E-E-H-H ... E-E-E-H-H*–like someone with old tennis shoes, but no matter how fast I tried to get away, they kept getting closer ... and *louder*. Then a plane swooped down at me, chasing me like Cary Grant in 'North by Northwest'!"

"Sounds like quite a nightmare. What happened next?"

"Whoever it was wrote *"Got you!"* on my shirt with a stick dipped in black slime and then blew *smoke* in my face! Then I woke up. Strange." Taylor shrugged and shoved another forkful of pancakes into her mouth.

"Probably just the new house, our late-night storm and visitor that were on your mind," Susan offered.

"And our wacky neighbor, Miss Peasy!"

"Taylor!"

"You mean an *old* house, Mom. An old, creepy, *creaky* house with a lot of dark spaces and cobwebs. Dad did a great job, but it gives me the crawls," Taylor said with a shudder. "It does make me want to learn its history, though, all that has

happened here over the past–how long's it been–
170 years?"

"Give or take. Me, too," Susan said between
sips of coffee, yawns, and glances out the kitchen
window. "We can do some research at the library.
Hey, here comes your new friend."

"Bobbi Leigh?" Taylor asked.

"The one and only."

"Mom, can I–"

"Go to the cave? I don't know, sweetie. Let's
ask Bobbi Leigh to tell us more about this cave.
Wouldn't hurt to find out more about *her*, don't
you think? I mean, a twelve-year-old roaming dark
and stormy roads alone at one-thirty in the
morning, parents not home? Begs some questions,
I should think! She's at the door. Want to go let
her in?"

"Okay."

Taylor crammed another forkful of pancake
rectangles into her mouth and guzzled it down with
milk.

"Hey, Mom, are parents all alike, like Bobbi Leigh says?"

"Hardly. Some parents are stricter than others. Maybe Bobbi Leigh's aren't as strict as she'd like. Maybe she thinks they're too strict, but that's nothing new!" Susan replied, taken off guard by the question. "Do you think I'm too strict?"

Taylor thought about the pros and cons of yes or no.

"Hard to say, really. Don't want to say something that might incriminate me."

"You think I'm too strict, don't you, Taylor?"

"She's here, Mom. We'll talk about this later."

Taylor ran toward the door, wiping her mouth with her sleeve and deftly sidestepping box after stacked box of unpacked household goods. Stacy pawed the door and sniffed the air seeping in at the doorjamb. Before Bobbi Leigh could lift the knocker and bring it down upon its brass plate, Taylor swung open the broad, heavy front door.

"Great nose ring!" Bobbi Leigh said in reference to the brass door knocker. "So, can you go?"

Bobbi Leigh pulled the screen door and helped herself into the house.

"Maybe," answered Taylor. "Mom wants to ask you some questions about it."

"Figures," said Bobbi Leigh with a sigh.

"Don't worry. My Mom's pretty cool about most stuff. She just likes to minimize the uncertainty, that's all."

"What the *what?*" Bobbi Leigh asked, stroking Stacy's hair. Nothing so disrupted Bobbi Leigh's train of thought than a string of unfamiliar words, most of which contained three or more syllables.

Taylor sighed. "She *hovers.* Come on, let's talk to her."

"Moms are moms, and Dads are Dads, all alike, no matter *what*," Bobbi Leigh declared. "They're just here to take away our fun, keep us under their thumb."

Taylor kept her tongue for the moment and did not disagree, not yet. Though Susan and Mike demanded discipline and order in the family routine, she didn't *feel* suppressed, if that was what Bobbi Leigh meant to suggest by "under their thumb".

Taylor had freedom, she believed, hard-earned and paid for with her responsible decisions. She had earned unsupervised excursions to, say, the movies now and then with her friends or hanging out at the mall, as long as Mom was in cell phone range.

But now that Bobbi Leigh had shone the light of attention upon the matter of parental subjugation, perhaps Susan *had* been overprotective these past several months. Actually for a *lot longer* than that, now that Taylor gave it deeper thought. The swimming incident in Middleboro came to mind. And that sleepover at Hannah's.

After all, adolescence was right around the corner. The time had come for some *serious*

breaking away! Or not. Thumbs had their
advantages, too.

"Under their thumb? Maybe. Maybe not."
whispered Taylor.

"Hey, nice bowl! Are you a woodturner?"
Bobbi Leigh asked as she stroked the flawless,
polished curve of a turned maple bowl.

"That's where you're wrong, Bobbi Leigh. My
Mom's cool; you'll see. And that's my Dad's bowl;
he's the woodturner ... or was, that is. Wait'll you
see his other woodturnings. They're still packed."

"Looks like most *everything* is still packed,"
Bobbi Leigh observed.

Taylor smiled but kept walking. "We just *got*
here, last *evening*. We're not the *moving fairies*,
you know!"

"Y'all have a car?" Bobbi Leigh asked,
peeking out a window.

"Should be delivered today. It's a van."

"You should get a Land Rover!"

"I wish we had a Jeep, or maybe one of those
Smart Cars. Get it?"

"You could get smushed like a bug in one of those Smart Cars. But they *are* cute," Bobbi Leigh said as she lifted the flap of one of the boxes stacked in the Living Room and took a curious peek inside. "Get what?"

Taylor rolled her eyes.

The girls approached Susan, her face buried in the October issue of Home Manicure.

"Mom, remember Bobbi Leigh?" Taylor asked sarcastically.

"How could I *forget?* Hi, Bobbi Leigh," Susan said, a broad smile across her face. "Did you find Ifs, Ands, and Buts – that takes some getting used to – and get them walked before the rain?"

"Yes, ma'am."

"Hope you avoided the downpour. Home alone, still?"

"Until tomorrow. Dad's flying into Atlanta and should be home by five. He's an attorney and has important clients in Chicago. Snobs, everyone! If you ask *me*, that is."

Susan chuckled uncomfortably at Bobbi Leigh's bluntness. "What about your mom?"

"Monday, maybe Tuesday. She's an architect and designs some pretty hideous stuff. Grownups have the *weirdest* tastes. No offense, Mrs. Smart! I love *your* taste," Bobbi Leigh said as her eyes roamed from ceiling to floor to wall and back. "So, can Taylor go explore the cave with me?"

"Possibly, but first I'd like you to tell me about this cave. Sounds dangerous."

"Well, it's a cave like most caves, I guess, except it's a lot smaller and not so dangerous unless you don't have a flashlight and decent shoes. Let me give you the bullet points."

Bullet points? thought Susan. *From a 12-year-old?*

"Let's see, big hole in the side of Tucker's Mountain; stays a constant 55 degrees; a few stalactites and such, but they're mainly broken; damp and dark; it's a bat paradise, not for the skittish; and-"

"Did you say ... bats?" Taylor asked, her words riding an onset of dread.

"Yeah, bats. Lots of them. Don't worry. They only come out at dusk. During the day, they just *hang* around."

Bobbi Leigh awaited a response to her wit. None came.

"Oh, I'm not worried," Taylor lied. "Actually, I'd love to see them. *Cool!* Mom, can I go?"

"Just how *deep* is this cave? Is this cave well-explored and well-known by the community? On whose property is this cave?" Susan spoke of "this cave" as if *it* were the intruder.

"Mom, one at a time," Taylor said, a bit embarrassed by her mom's aggressive questioning."

"It's okay," Bobbi Leigh whispered, "I can handle them. This cave is a small one, barely big enough to throw a fit."

Bobbi Leigh paused, hoping again for a laugh. Not to be, she continued.

"Um, there are deeper ones around here, so I've heard, but I don't have permission for those. This one's on Sheriff Hagan's property, down by Lake Jasper. He lets me go in it all the time. It's not very deep, at least not the part I'm aware of. I'd guess ... a hundred feet, tops.

"I don't think people really explore this cave much anymore, if they ever did. I mean, it seems pretty lame as caves go. If it were *really* any good, it'd be all touristy and junk, with handrails and lights and those stupid souvenir shops. All the stalactites – not many to begin with – have been broken off – souvenirs, you know – and the artifacts are mostly gone, I think."

"Artifacts? What kind of artifacts?" Susan asked.

"I dunno. The Indian kind, I guess. You know, arrowheads and pottery, stuff like that. Sheriff Hagan's got tons of artifacts, all collected from that cave, he says. Anyway, I've never found any. Never really looked for them."

"Is it okay to go, Mom? You seem more hesitant about this *cave* than you did about Miss Peasy's flight credentials."

Susan gazed into Taylor's pleading eyes. Susan needed some alone time to complete the Christmas article for the December edition of Home Manicure magazine.

"Wait until *you're* a mom, sweetie."

"So you've met our Miss Peasy: pilot, carpenter, and all-around nutjob?" Bobbi Leigh asked.

Susan stood shocked at Bobbi Leigh's blunt, disrespectful assessment.

"Met her yesterday. *Is* she a pilot, Bobbi Leigh?" Susan asked, instantly diverted from talk of caves. "What can you share with us about her?"

"A pilot? I guess. So she says, but who can believe what *she* says? I mean, what's an 89-year-old doing flying any airplane anyhow?"

"Have you seen her airplane, Bobbi Leigh?" asked Susan.

"Oh, yes, I've *seen* it. Sparkles like a polished *diamond*. More a trophy than a plane. Somebody keeps that plane spotless. If you ask me, I don't think it's ever been off the ground."

"So you've never actually seen her fly this plane of hers?"

"Didn't I just say that? Naw. She says so, but I ain't never seen her fly it. But, then, I don't go to the airport often, either. Only when I have a mind to ride my bike out that way. Show you her pilot's license, did she?"

"She did. Looked authentic enough. Is … isn't it?"

"I guess so. I've seen it, too, and it looks official, but it don't take much these days to pull a head fake. I've seen one of the deputies come pick her up now and again and take her someplace, the airport maybe, grocery shopping, who knows. She don't drive."

"Where's the airport, Bobbi Leigh?" Taylor asked.

"More of an air*strip*, really. It's a long, flat field near the base of Sagitaw Falls. Ain't never more than three airplanes there at any one time, I'm told. Climbers mostly use it to park their cars and climb up the cliffs near the falls."

Susan thought a moment about Bobbi Leigh's information.

"Okay, well, check your flashlight for batteries," Susan answered with a sigh.

"Yes!" Taylor responded, arm pumping the air.

Bobbi Leigh patted her pocket. "Got *my* flashlight, right here. It's a 250-lumen SureShot Sentinel, perfect for caves! See?" Bobbi Leigh flicked on the flashlight, tilted at the perfect angle to catch Susan's eyes head on.

"Yikes! Now *that's* bright!" Susan exclaimed, shielding her eyes.

"Sorry, Mrs. Smart! You bet it's bright! 250 lumens bright!"

"Lumens? What exactly are lumens?" Susan asked.

"Beats me, Mrs. Smart. Something to do with brightness, which this baby has plenty of! I think one lumen is as bright as one candle, unless you've got one of those really *big* candles that creates *big* flames. Those're probably worth five lumens each. Maybe one birthday candle equals one lumen," Bobbi Leigh said, over-explaining, cupping her chin in her fingers and tilting her head upward. "All I know is that this little guy will light up that whole cave!"

Taylor ran to the hall closet and pulled from a box one of three flashlights. She clicked it on. A circle of light brightened the closet wall. *Probably only 50 lumens*, she thought.

"Good to go, Mom!" she shouted.

"I'm still a little concerned about this cave business, Taylor."

"Mom. I'm practically a teenager."

Susan sighed as she pushed Taylor's tangle of morning hair off her shoulders. "Okay. You can go."

"Yes!" Taylor repeated, fist clinched.

"I need to finish this article by two thirty. But I expect you home by three o'clock, no later. We've got more work to do in this house than I care to think about. That gives you *six hours*, ample time. I'm going to call Sheriff Hagan and let him know you're going to the cave. Before you go anywhere, Taylor, let's make a few sandwiches; you two're going to need them. Peanut butter and jelly okay with you, Bobbi Leigh?"

"Got strawberry?" Bobbi Leigh answered.

"Got blackberry preserves and grape jelly."

"Grape, I guess."

"Blackberry for me, Mom."

Susan pulled a loaf of bread, peanut butter, and a fresh jar of grape jelly from a shopping bag of road supplies. "By the way, Bobbi Leigh, how does one get to this cave?"

"Lake Jasper is three and a half miles down the road, that way," Bobbi Leigh answered. "The paved road becomes dirt and heads north at the lake. You'll see a big cedar tree on the right, a few hundred yards down the dirt road. Cave's on the north side of that tree. Can't miss it. You'll see our bikes."

"Good day for a bike ride, after all that rain last night," Susan said.

"Craziest fall weather I've ever seen around here!"

Susan packed four sandwiches and two bottles of water in Taylor's backpack.

"Thanks, Mom!" Taylor said, giving Susan a hug. "I'll be back by three, promise."

"Have fun, and-"

"I know, *be careful!*" Taylor said with a roll of her eyes, finishing her mom's oft-repeated instruction. "I will."

"Parents pretty much worry all the time around here," Bobbi Leigh said.

"Worry? Why is that, Bobbi Leigh?" Susan asked.

"Oh, I don't know. Legends and rumors and stuff, maybe. Most of Raventon's parents just always seem to be on edge, to worry. The thing that gets them the most is something about a story of some kids that went missing here a couple of hundred years ago, just before Raventon was officially founded. And then there were those other kids, just last year. That one's real."

"Some kids went ... *missing?*" Taylor asked, looking at her mom and thinking of her dad.

9

The Witch of Raventon

"The 200-year-old set of missing kids is just a legend," Bobbi Leigh said with a dismissive shrug, "but as legends go, it's a pretty good one for campfires and such. It didn't *really* happen, though. At least I don't *think* it did; not as it's told, anyway. You know how legends are. Stuff's added here, taken away there, exaggerated. Besides, it's ancient history."

"What can you tell us about this legend, Bobbi Leigh," Susan asked, "and the more *recent* set of missing kids?"

"Mom. Not now. The clock's ticking, you know."

"It'll just take a minute, sweetie. Tell us, Bobbi Leigh."

Bobbi Leigh gave Taylor that familiar parents-are-all-alike glance and a smile.

"Well–and remember, this is *just* a legend– some kids, ten of them, I believe, hiked up Tucker's Mountain, near where the lake is now, one autumn morning, kind of like today, to pick berries or flowers or whatever kids picked two hundred years ago. The day started off sunny and mild, but storm clouds rolled in just after noon.

"Only these weren't just *any* storm clouds. Turned out to be the worst tornado this town's ever seen, they say. Very unusual weather for autumn. Practically destroyed everything in Raventon, they say, not that there was a whole lot in Raventon to destroy in those days."

Susan and Taylor stood as still as posts, eyes and ears fixed on Bobbi Leigh.

"Anyway, those kids never came back; nobody ever saw them alive again. People searched and searched for them on the mountain but never found a trace; only a wide swath of ripped up trees and debris. Until one day the following spring. That's when stuff started to show up, *weird* stuff."

"What … stuff?" Taylor asked.

"You know, *stuff*, the missing kids' stuff. The kids' clothes they'd worn the day of the tornado, for example, were found hung on porch posts and doorknobs; things they'd taken with them on their hike, toys and pails, stuff they would have had to carry, stuff that wouldn't have just *blown* into town on the wind, unless that wind happened to be another tornado, which it wasn't. Or maybe it was; who knows."

Bobbi Leigh touched a piece of blown glass on a shelf, examining its swirls of colors, as she continued telling.

"Other things, weird things, things they didn't even take with them on the hike, things like books–and not just *any* books–scary storybooks *nobody* in Raventon owned, so they claim, and family bibles, even cookware from the homes of these same ten kids! Somebody piled these things up in the middle of Raventon's main street, one by one, day after day, and nobody ever saw anybody doing the piling."

"What happened next?" Taylor asked.

"Somebody–nobody knows who–set torch to the pile one night, just put it afire and burned it right up. Folks tried to put out the fire, but despite buckets of water and sand, it kept burning until all that remained of the pile were ashes, like some *sacrifice!* After that, it stopped."

"It stopped? You mean all this just stopped?"

"Dead in its tracks. No more mysterious stuff or weird piles of anything. No more people missing; nothing. They blamed it all on the Witch of Raventon."

"The *Witch of Raventon?*" Taylor asked.

"Time passed and people stopped remembering. They didn't *forget*, mind you. They just didn't want to remember. Eventually, the facts–whatever the facts–were replaced by lore and legend, tales handed down generation to generation, and nobody's seen nothing like it since, end of story."

All were silent for a moment.

"Well, maybe not quite end of story. Some say the Raventon Witch is alive and well to this day, living *right here* in town." Bobbi Leigh added.

"Okay," Susan finally blurted. "Good thing that legend is just that, a legend."

"Mom, there's truth in all legends," Taylor noted. Bobbi Leigh nodded in agreement.

"Bobbi Leigh, you mentioned some other kids, from last year. What happened?"

"Oh, that. Just some kids went missing again, but not from here. This happened in the next county, and they found those kids safe and sound. Lost hiking for three days. It just put folks to mind of the legend of Tucker's Mountain and got them all riled again. Ready to go, Tay?"

"Me?" Taylor asked, pointing to herself.

"Of course, you! Like it? The shortened name, that is."

"I guess." Taylor wasn't sure about the truncated name, but she did feel more accepted. "Yeah, it's cool, I suppose." Both girls smiled. "Let's go. See ya, Mom. Back by three."

Taylor and Bobbi Leigh slung their backpacks over their shoulders, strapped on their helmets, and mounted their bikes.

"Be careful!" Susan shouted as the two girls pedaled down the road. "Watch for cars! I'm giving Sheriff Hagan a call!"

Susan watched the girls until they disappeared around a curve. She pulled her cell phone from her pocket and punched in the number for the Sheriff's office.

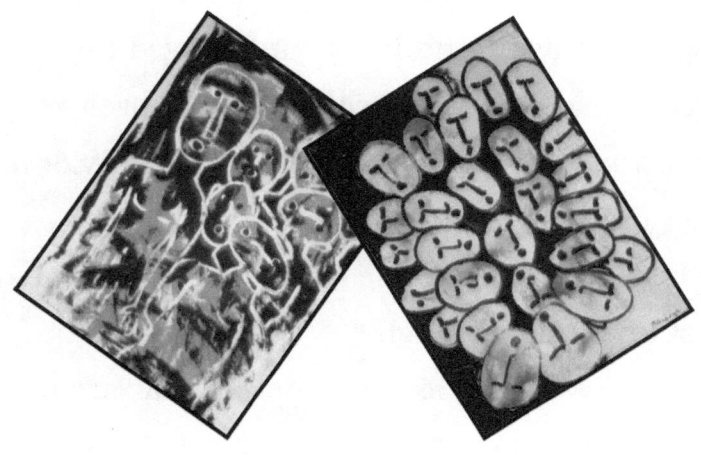

10

A Closet of Skeletons

"If you can't get rid of the skeletons in your closet, you'd best teach them to dance."

- George Bernard Shaw

"Sheriff's office, how may I help you?"

"Sheriff Hagan, please," Susan replied.

"Sheriff Hagan is out on a call. Could I be of assistance?" the dispatcher asked.

"Yes, maybe so. This is Susan Smart. My daughter, Taylor, and I have just moved to Raventon; got here yesterday. We live over on Shadowood, on the east side. Anyway, Taylor and a very quick-found friend-"

"Let me guess," the dispatcher interrupted. "First name Bobbi Leigh?"

"Yes," Susan replied, one eyebrow arched, "how did you know?"

"When you've lived in Raventon a few years, Mrs. Smart, you won't ask that question."

"Anyway, Taylor and Bobbi Leigh set out on their bikes for Lake Jasper a few minutes ago and are planning to explore some little cave over there. It's my understanding the cave is on Sheriff Hagan's property and, according to Bobbi Leigh, is okay to explore. I wanted to confirm this with him."

"I'll give him the message, ma'am, but as far as I know, Sheriff Hagan doesn't own land by Lake Jasper. And I'm not aware of a cave."

"I see," Susan replied, surprised by this unexpected information.

"But, not to worry. Lake Jasper is public land, as is Tucker's Mountain and all the land around the lake. Sort of a de facto state park, you see, though not officially designated as such. Lots of folks visit up there, and it wouldn't surprise me if there *were* caves up there in those limestone hills. I just don't pay much attention to that sort of thing. I'll give the Sheriff your message. Want him to call you back, ma'am?"

"Yes. Please ask him to call me as soon as he's able," Susan responded as she gazed down the road before re-entering the house. "My number is 555-7013."

"Thank you, ma'am. And welcome to Raventon. I don't mean to pry, ma'am, but didn't you move into the old Hatcher place?"

"That's right. But now it's the old *Smart* place. Beautiful house. Loads of character and history that smacks one like … well, like one of Miss Peasy's apple pies!"

Susan deduced that if the dispatcher knew of Bobbi Leigh, she knew even more of Miss Peasy.

"We gained title to the house six years ago and vowed to restore its original architecture, inside and out," Susan said proudly, "plus some modernizations, all of which he has done."

"I'm not much on this sort of thing, ma'am," the dispatcher said in a measured cadence, "but folks believe ... that is, they *say* that place is *one haunted house.*"

"*Haunted?*"

"Now, just so you know, I don't believe in spooks and such, but some of the *stories* that people tell! That sort of thing makes my skin tingle!"

"Stories? Such as ..."

"Well, I really shouldn't carry on like this," the dispatcher said, lowering her voice to a near-whisper, "but people say that Colonel Smart murdered his family, a wife and two sons, right after the war, right in *that house* you've moved into."

"Murdered? Oh my ... When did *this* happen? World War two?" Susan asked.

Mike had not shared this tidbit of morbid family history with his wife and daughter. Susan listened.

"No, the War between the States, back in the spring of 1865. Henry Smart was promoted to Colonel and transferred into Lee's Army of Northern Virginia in 1862 after having enlisted in the 22nd Georgia the spring of 1861. There, he commanded the 18th Virginia Volunteers and was part of Pettigrew's command in Pickett's Charge at Gettysburg. You probably already know all of this, so just feel free to stop me.

"Anyway, he was a proud Southerner, the Colonel was, and had built that house in 1843 with his own two hands. He hated slavery, and no record shows he ever owned a one. He made his fortune in lumber and gave his political loyalty first to his state and then to the new country that followed.

Mark Randolph Watters

"He formed the Raventon Volunteer Rifles before his transfer to Lee and eventually fought with Lee not only at Gettysburg but against Grant's Overland Campaign in Virginia, losing an arm at the Wilderness and an eye at Spotsylvania.

"After the surrender, he made it home to Raventon, a beaten man in a beaten town. This is where this story gets interesting. While convalescing from slow-healing wounds and a bout with malaria, Colonel Smart learned that his sons had survived the war but had done so wearing *Yankee* uniforms in *Grant's* army.

"Story goes that he knew his sons were mustered into a company formed near Dalton, but he'd lost track of their whereabouts. He found out a year later that they were captured near Fredericksburg. What he did not know was that instead of being shipped to a northern prison, they were given the chance of freedom *if* they pledged an oath of loyalty to the Union ... and *if* they joined the Yankee army.

Taylor Smart and the Chamber of Skulls

"He could stand a lot of things, the Colonel, but betrayal was not one of them, which, of course, was all he could feel, don't you see, especially after he believed with all his being that his own flesh and blood were loyal to the Confederacy. He convinced himself it was his *sons* who had taken his arm in the Wilderness and his eye at Spotsylvania.

"Well, you can imagine his rage," the dispatcher continued. "One arm or no, he found the strength to hack them to death–wife, too–with the very Bowie knife he'd carried as a side arm into battle.

"They say that knife's still in the house somewhere, planted under a floorboard or behind a wall, bloodied still. His was the only public hanging this town's ever seen. Folks say their ghosts roam that old house to this day. Folks say they hear screams in the *dead of night* coming from those upstairs rooms, the kind of screams that make you wish you'd never been born. Have you heard any such goings-on in that house yet, Mrs. Smart?"

Susan picked up Stacy and held her close as she listened. She thought about the strange creaking sounds she and Taylor had heard the night before.

"Wow. What a story! Well, the house *is* old, and noises are bound to happen in old houses like this," Susan observed.

"I suppose," the dispatcher answered. "But I'm talking about *screams*. There's a big difference between screams and a house settling. Like I said, ma'am, I don't mean to pry, but ... didn't your husband die in that house."

Susan paused, careful in her response. "No, not in the house. And nobody's absolutely certain he's dead. I mean, he's been missing almost a year now. The authorities *presume* he's dead, but until they find his body-"

"But they found a grave, didn't they? And clothes?"

Susan's discomfort grew with each nosy question.

"He's just *missing*, that's all."

"Poor fellow. I'm so sorry for your loss, Mrs. Smart. I remember seeing him around town. He seemed the picture of health, jogging over all these hills. Handsome devil, too! He made that old house something worth looking at. Brought back its original *grandeur*, as they say!"

Susan was not ready to concede her "loss", and she found it disturbing that others in Raventon considered the matter fodder for the gossip fence.

"Thank you. It truly is a lovely old house."

"Good things have happened there, too, Mrs. Smart."

"Such as?"

Susan believed the dispatcher's knowledge trumped whatever resources the library might possess. She listened for an answer.

"Well, seems the Hatchers–that's the family that supposedly bought the house from the city of

Raventon after the Smart murders–had some ties to James Garfield." The dispatcher paused for Susan's reaction but got none. "He was our 20th President, elected back in 1880, I believe it was.

"Anyway, the Hatchers had ties to the president, childhood friends, I'm told. Newly-elected President Garfield made a trip to Raventon in early June of 1881, a month before he was shot, to attend a dinner party hosted by the Hatchers. Raventon was fit to be tied, a President visiting and all!

"Folks say that old house is responsible for Garfield's assassination, sort of a curse. Of course, as with spooks, I don't much fall in line with curses either. Besides, how can it be a curse when Raventon has benefitted so wonderfully from a Presidential visit locked in its history?

"But you should also know that before Garfield's visit, even before the murders, General Sherman had used the house briefly as his headquarters during the great unpleasantness. That's where that man put the finishing touches on his March-to-the-Sea plans and extended his thanks to the citizens of Raventon by setting torch to the town. Except the Shadowood area, that is."

Susan detected a hint of resentment in the dispatcher's tone.

"Maybe *that* was the foundation for the curse. If one believed in curses, of course. Anyway, I have taken *way* too much of your time, Mrs. Smart. Please forgive me."

"Not at all," Susan replied, having no previous knowledge of such events. "I appreciate the information and the history lesson. Thanks again. Goodbye."

"One more thing," the dispatcher shouted as Susan's finger touched, but did not press, the 'end call' button.

"Yes?"

"Don't know if you know this, but some folks say ownership of the house was never *legally* transferred when the Hatchers sold it back to Mike's great-grandparents. Something about ... what was it ... the incomplete exchange of consideration, or some legal mumbo-jumbo. Anyway, Mrs. Smart, that was then, and I'm sure that if there was any truth to that, you'd know all about it by now."

"Thanks. Thank you," Susan said, her voice stumbling. "You've been most helpful. Oh ..."

"Yes, Mrs. Smart."

"What ... what can you tell me about Peasy Parlevous?"

"Miss Peasy? A bit eccentric, perhaps, but salt of the earth. Met her?"

"Yes, we're neighbors."

"Well, consider yourself lucky. She's steady of hand and firm of mind, not to mention the best cook in all of Raventon. Besides, anyone who has made it to eighty-nine and still flies her own airplane - cropdusts at that - has earned the right to be as eccentric as she likes, don't you think?"

"Of course, you're right. She *cropdusts?*"

"Every second Wednesday."

Miss Peasy's list of eccentricities grew longer.

"Thanks again!"

Susan ended the call and tucked her phone into her pocket. *Cropdusts? Maybe Miss Peasy's the genuine article after all.* She scanned the grand heights of the great room's ceiling, its glinting brass chandelier staring down at her with its empty candle holders.

*If **they** could talk,* she thought. *House not legally transferred? Mike never mentioned anything like that.*

Shaking her head, Susan glanced at her watch and said, "Got to get on that article!"

Mark Randolph Watters

11

Irving Legend

"Common sense is genius dressed in its working clothes."

-- Emerson

The pedal to Lake Jasper took the girls quickly from the clatter of town and into the rural realm of willow-winding switchbacks and mud-filled stretches of straight road shaded by canopies of thick oaks and sycamores, mixed on occasion with a longleaf pine, all clothed in shawls of kudzu.

*This really **is** the stuff of legends*, thought Taylor as they weaved around potholes and stones and glided through shadowy hollows. *The headless horseman would have **loved** this place!*

"Speaking of *legends*," Taylor shouted, "this ride is like an *Irving* Legend!" Some of her dad's wordplay had rubbed off on Taylor.

"A *what?*" Bobbi Leigh replied, whisking blown hair from her mouth. "Don't you mean an *urban* legend?"

"Never mind."

"Whatever."

Tortured branches twisted over the road, as if with the mind to gnarl their way toward bikers and pluck them straight from their seats. Tree knots and trunk holes stared with the bony silence of eyeless skulls.

The morning sun warmed the air gradually and gave way to mid-morning thunderheads bubbling about the sky. Rumbles rolled on breaking waves of air, weakened by distance but nonetheless producing enough noise to announce a storm's imminent arrival.

As the girls emerged into a clearing, Taylor scanned the sky, hoping these scattered, menacing masses of charcoal gray clouds managed somehow to miss them, to "go around us", borrowing her grandparents' folksy assessment of such weather phenomena, as if storms had minds of their own, like migrating flocks of ravens or gnarly tree branches.

"Looks like we're in for it!" shouted Bobbi Leigh as the girls coasted down a welcomed slope.

"Yeah. Let's hope it goes around us!"

"Goes around us? Not in Raventon, not likely. Storms pretty much like it here!"

"*Like* it here? You think so?" Taylor replied, reconsidering the possibility of storms with minds of their own.

"Why not? Don't *you* like it here? Storms seem to. One pops up just about everyday. Wettest summer and fall I can remember! Something about mountains and air pressure and lift and El uh-ohs and science junk that bores me to tears."

Bobbi Leigh slammed on her breaks and skidded sideways to a halt, kicking up sprays of grit and scattering pebbles. Taylor did the same in quick response, more to avoid bowling over Bobbi Leigh.

"Lake's around that bend ahead," Bobbi Leigh said, panting. "It's not all that big, but people come from everywhere to canoe and fish here. Rainbow trout or something like that, from the Sagitaw River. Bass, maybe? I wouldn't know. A fish is a fish to me, and they're *all* yucky, on a **scale** of one to yuck."

Bobbi Leigh paused for maximum comedic effect. Instead, Taylor tilted her head and closed one eye. Clearing her throat, Bobbi Leigh continued.

"Anyway, it's a good takeout point for canoeists and kayakers. That I *do* know. See that? Of course you see it; how can you *not* see it! That's Tucker's Mountain. That's where the cave is! Come on!"

Bobbi Leigh pedaled faster. Taylor found it difficult to keep pace with Bobbi Leigh's mountain-bred physical fitness.

Taylor Smart and the Chamber of Skulls

"Wait up!" Taylor shouted, wriggling her shoulders to adjust backpack straps. Like crazed pistons, her legs pumped the pedals of her single-speed bike.

Lake Jasper was Raventon's principal water source, a reservoir built in the early 1900s to capture and hold water from the Sagitaw River. It also captured runoff from surrounding streams and directly off the slopes of Tucker's Mountain, a 2,500-foot-elevation peak and a hiker magnet. The lake's depths ranged from a few feet near the eastern shoreline to several hundred feet at its southern, earthen-dammed end where most boating enthusiasts congregated.

A half-mile hike from Lake Jasper, Sagitaw Falls thundered out of Tucker's Mountain, dropping four hundred and seventy-two feet down the sheer northern cliffs. The fall's picturesque drop and pounding cascades beckoned photographers, rappellers, and hikers. Spelunkers had not yet discovered the area's underground wonders, but that was only a matter of time.

Caves of varying depths dotted the base of Tucker's Mountain at Lake Jasper, though none was considered a sufficient challenge to attract thrill seekers.

One cave in particular, an opening at least ten feet in diameter and curtained partially by kudzu and honeysuckle, was Bobbi Leigh's destination. This cave was isolated from the view of lake swimmers and the path of falls-focused hikers. The girls pedaled past the activity of the lake and toward the obscurity of the cave area.

The roar of Sagitaw Falls, though a half-mile away, joined the approaching thunderhead in a concerto of nature's power, an antithesis to the calm of Taylor's beloved chamber music. Like an orchestral climax punctuated by cymbals and tympanis, the crescendo caught Taylor in a wisp of remembrance.

12

The Cave

"The mystery is what prompted men to leave caves, to come out of the womb of nature."

-- Stephen Gardiner

"There she is, Tay!" Bobbi Leigh shouted, pointing straight ahead. "Let's drop our bikes here."

"Where?" Taylor asked, shielding her eyes from the sun's glare.

"Here! Drop your bike right *here*."

"No, I mean the cave! How can you *tell?*"

"I just know! See that batch of kudzu?
Cave's right there; trust me!"

Taylor glared at the steep mountainside, its
wall of foliage the perfect camouflage. She scanned
the wall searching for an obvious hole that
screamed, "CAVE!", maybe even a "Beware of Bats"
sign, anything that might help her feel a little less
blind. Of course, nothing so convenient existed
except flora visited now and again by flitting dots of
sulfur butterflies bouncing from one spider lily to
the next.

"Follow me, Tay!"

Bobbi Leigh led Taylor along a narrow
footpath toward the cave's entrance. Taylor felt a
significant dip in air temperature as they
approached the entrance, the blackness of which
was now apparent to Taylor behind streams of
twisting vines.

"Come on! Over *here!*" Bobbi Leigh directed,
excited to show Taylor another slice of her world.
"Watch your step, low ceiling. Don't step in that

puddle of water; it's deeper than it looks.
Stalagmite to your left. Whoa, spider web at twelve
o'clock!"

Cool! thought Taylor, her head bobbing like a
fishing cork in reaction to Bobbi Leigh's flurry of
warnings. *A real cave!* Even her *thoughts* seemed
to echo.

"It's pretty ordinary in this part," Bobbi Leigh
explained, shining her 250-lumen SureShot
Sentinel onto the walls, exposing – startling – a few
resting bats, "but wait'll we get a little farther.
Right here is what I call the Cathedral."

Taylor gasped, seeing nothing at all ordinary
about the sights. The girls were standing in an
underground room as big as an auditorium, its
ceiling twice as high. Ancient formations of broken
stalactites and stalagmites, ravaged by visitors
past, covered the ceiling and floor, most resembling
sawed branches and tree trunks. Only the thickest
survived human pummeling.

"Check this out, Tay!" Bobbi Leigh shouted,
as she approached a stalagmite.

"Takes about two hundred years for one of these things to grow an *inch*," Taylor observed, running her finger over its smooth surface, "and only a couple of seconds to destroy that process."

"You seem to know about cave stuff."

"Some, I guess," Taylor replied. "Books, the Geographics, trips to Carlsbad ... you know. Limestone caves like this one are full of these things. Water seeps through the ground, dissolving the limestone and carrying it along until it drips to the floor. Some of the dissolved limestone stays at the ceiling and the rest drops to the floor. Over time–a *whole lot* of time, two hundred years per inch–these things form."

"There's a passageway to the left, a couple of hundred feet beyond that cluster of boulders, that I've not explored yet," Bobbi Leigh said, pointing. "Sheriff Hagan said to keep away from any passageway we might find leading out of the Great Room, except the entrance of course. Wanna check it out anyway?" Bobbi Leigh cast the glow of her 250 lumens upon the cluster.

"But I thought you said–"

"Who *cares* what I said!"

"Okay, then, I thought *Sheriff Hagan* said to stay away from passageways."

"So he did. So *what!* Tay, we're practically *teenagers* now. I think we can manage. Besides, if it's big enough to get through, who knows what we might find ... *beyond the wall!*" Bobbi Leigh spoke with spooky emphasis, wiggling her spidery fingers, as if she were narrating a movie trailer. "More artifacts, maybe."

"But, the Sheriff–"

"Sheriff, *shmeriff,* are you *with* me or not?"

"With you, I guess. I mean ... *sure,* let's do it!" Taylor said with a shrug, trying to stifle her nagging common sense, as well as her incessant obedience to authority, a rule her dad insisted she follow. "Do you think it's safe?"

"Only one way to find out. You're not ... *scared,* are you?"

"Scared? *Me?* Wild horses couldn't keep me away, not even wild *bats!* Full steam ahead, I always say!"

Bobbi Leigh looked at Taylor with curled lips of skepticism.

"Right. Anyway, it'll give us something to talk about during show-and-tell on Tuesday. Watch your step. Rocks get slippery."

Flashlight in hand, Taylor maneuvered around and over the smooth, water-slicked rocks as she followed Bobbi Leigh, occasionally resorting to a posture resembling the limbo for negotiating around and between tight groups of low-hanging stalactites and rock curtains.

The girls struggled to push aside the group of several small boulders, just enough to clear the passage entrance. The forbidden passageway, a rough circle of a couple of feet in diameter, allowed entry only by crawling. Cool air spilled from its mouth, as if fan-blown, making a monotonous droning sound, like that of a midnight wind through a cemetery. Shallow pools of cold water covered the floor.

"Gonna have to crawl through," Bobbi Leigh said, "on our bellies."

"You first," Taylor said with a smile.

"Okay, then, let's go," Bobbi Leigh said as she pocketed her fancy flashlight. "On second thought, Tay, use my light. We'll need every lumen."

"By the way, it's *Muley*," Taylor said.

"What'd you say? Muley? Did you say ... *Muley?*

"I did. Call me Muley, my nickname. Friends back home called me that. Dad gave it to me."

"Your *dad* did that to you?"

"It's not something he *did* to me! You make it sound like a voodoo spell or something. It's a long story. I'll tell you all about it someday. At first I hated it too – anyone would, I reckon – but then it sort of *grew* on me."

"Like mold on bread, I'm guessing!" said Bobbi Leigh.

"Very funny; my sides are splitting. Look, it's because I'm *stubborn*. You know, like a *mule*. You'll get used to it. I did."

Bobbi Leigh stared a moment at Taylor, thinking *Are you for real?* She considered Taylor and her nickname in the same fashion a gopher might consider concrete for digging – they just don't *go* together!

"Anyway ... Muley ... my light's more powerful. Keep it shining through the passageway. That's right, like that."

Taylor struggled to keep the flow of light above Bobbi Leigh's head. What little both could see ahead, given the inconsistency of the coverage of the bobbing light, looked innocuous enough, as opposed to the absolute terror of total darkness. The two-foot space opened by the passageway soon narrowed by nearly half, then widened, twisting this way and that, like a section of an amusement park spook house. The girls intermittently crawled on their knees or squirmed on their stomachs, each inch forward soaking a bit more dampness into their clothing.

"Point the light to the ground ahead of me, *Tay!*"

As would a gopher with concrete, Bobbi Leigh rejected the 'Muley' moniker.

"Point the light!" Bobbi Leigh repeated and then followed with a whisper, "but shed the 'Muley'!"

"I'm pointing, I'm *pointing! You* try crawling with a 250-lumen flashlight in *your* hand!"

"Sorry. I just need to see if there are any pits, puddles, holes or other things best avoided."

"Can't hold it properly. Too narrow a space. I can't lift the flashlight above my head and shine it over yours. And I'm not shedding the Muley."

"You heard?"

"I heard. Acoustics are *great* in here!"

"Acoustics? What are ... never mind!"

Bobbi Leigh reached back and, in a motion of sheer will, grabbed her flashlight from Taylor. She rested it against a stone, tilting it upward.

"Ceiling's high enough to stand just ahead. *Whoa!* Check out *those* stalactites!"

The girls emerged from the tight crawl space, into a room larger than they imagined. On their knees, they wiped grit and dirt from their pants and tried drying their hands on wet shirts. They raised slowly, hands instinctively above their heads, to ward off renegade rocks. Standing stiff as stones, they stared at what the light revealed.

"These formations are *undisturbed*, Muley. Man, that Muley thing *is* going to take some getting *used* to!" Bobbi Leigh said, shaking her head as if she'd taken in a whiff of dung. "Do you realize we–you and me–have got to be the *first ever* to explore this section of the cave! Are you *hearing* me?"

Taylor heard fine but was distracted by another sound.

"I hear water up ahead," Taylor said. She cupped her ear. "A *lot* of water. Sounds like falls."

"Could be, I suppose. Maybe it's an underground river! Let's scope out this room first. Watch out for stalactites; some of them are pretty sharp, enough so to put holes in the heads of stubborn *mules*."

Taylor placed one hand on her hip and, giving Bobbi Leigh a smirky stare, pointed her flashlight toward the ceiling, revealing a colorful array of rock formations, undisturbed through the depths of time.

She and Bobbi Leigh maneuvered over the boulder-strewn floor and through narrow wall openings. They had found a whole new section of what Bobbi Leigh previously believed to be an ordinary, hardly-impressive cave.

Remarkably high, as much as a hundred feet in places, the ceiling covered rooms as spacious as gymnasia. Stalagmites arose from the ground, like leafless rock cacti, some meeting with stalactites to form magnificent hourglass-shaped stone columns. The bases of some of the stalagmites glistened, like monuments wet with polish. Stalactites hung from the ceiling, some as tiny as straws, drops of cold water occasionally falling from their tips leaving behind microscopic deposits of minerals, each drop a minuscule contribution to a timeless process.

"Wow! Look over *here*, Bobbi Leigh!" Taylor shouted. "Oh my *gosh!*"

Bobbi Leigh looked, gasped, and swallowed. "Looks like ... maybe we're *not* the first!"

13

Sheriff Hagan

"A wolf in sheep's clothing ..."

- Aesop

"Aaaah!" Susan screamed. "I have *got* to change that!"

Like the reaction of one's leg when a doctor's hammer strikes the patellar tendon, her arms sprawled reflexively, sending dozens of neatly stacked papers flying. Mozart's Serenade Number 13, the ring tone on her cell phone, had abruptly interrupted the focus of her proofreading.

"Sheriff Hagan!" Susan answered, scrambling to retrieve the scattered papers and her composure. "Thanks for returning my call."

"Glad to, Mrs. Smart. And welcome to Raventon. What can I do for you?"

"Thank you, Sheriff. Good to be here, though I wish the circumstances were different."

"I understand, Mrs. Smart."

"Anyway, my daughter, Taylor, and a friend she met last night – her name's Bobbi Leigh – have biked up to Lake Jasper this morning, to explore a cave in Tucker's Mountain. Bobbi Leigh said this cave was on your property, that it was safe, and that you would be okay with them exploring it. I just wanted to touch base with you and confirm."

"They're exploring the cave? Well ... okay," Sheriff Hagan replied with hesitance, his tone hinting this might not be the safest activity for two 12-year-old girls.

"Is there a problem, Sheriff? I knew I should have waited and talked to you first!"

"No, no, Mrs. Smart, it's okay, really, it is. The cave's safe, as far as I know, but it's not on my property. It's *adjacent* to my property, but the State owns the lake, the cave, and most of the mountain. Some politicians campaigned a few years back about making it a state park, but nothing came of it, politics of the situation being what they were.

"Nobody much goes to that cave anyhow, far as I know. Not much of a tourist attraction up there, being mostly hidden by vegetation and without the usual touristy signage and souvenir shops. Just ain't been developed. Not likely to be, either.

"Besides, I've posted a "Keep Out" sign, just to discourage outsiders from venturing in. I'm sure those girls are okay. I know Bobbi Leigh pretty well, and she's a straight-and-narrow kind of girl, risk-averse, if you know what I mean; though one might not think so on first impression. They can't get very far inside anyway."

Susan paused, somewhat skeptical. The Bobbi Leigh she'd met didn't seem the risk-averse type at all.

"So, you've explored it?" asked Susan.

"I have, years ago as a boy, mainly. Found a lot of Indian left-behinds in that cave. Arrowheads, knives, pottery, hammerstones, axes, stuff like that. Even found some petroglyphs. Seems more of a rock shelter, actually, than a cave."

"Petroglyphs? What are petroglyphs?" Susan asked.

"Cave drawings. Prehistoric people scratched pictures into the rock walls and boulders. One of their ways of communicating, I suppose. Some of it is quite artistic, in an impressionistic sort of way; some of it seems to portray a record of everyday life for those people; and some of it is nothing short of mysterious."

"Mysterious? How so?"

"Hard to say, really," Sheriff Hagan replied. "For me, if I can't figure something out, it's mysterious!"

"I know what you mean, Sheriff!"

"Some of the drawings are concentric circles and other odd shapes; human stick figures chasing other human stick figures; abstractions of animals and humans, perhaps depicting a hunt; human and animal skulls, things like that, battles maybe. Don't know if they were artists or just bored. Obviously the creators knew exactly what the drawings were about, but as for us, well, they'll remain a mystery."

"These people lived in that cave? How easy was *that!* Ready-made house! Nothing to renovate; just show up and set up!"

Susan thought about the mountain of unpacking ahead.

"Perhaps, Mrs. Smart, but nothing about their lives was easy. While master hunters, certainly, they were too often the hunted as well, easily overwhelmed by predators, even by other roaming bands of Natives, themselves looking for a "ready-made" house.

"I tried getting the University's archaeologists to survey the cave for possible excavation, but you know how that goes, funding and such. No telling what's still in that cave or when it might be discovered."

"Sounds like the cave of a child's dreams," Susan observed.

"And it *was!* Wouldn't surprise me a bit if those girls come out of there with backpacks full of left-behinds."

Left-behinds. That's what Mike called them. Susan chuckled at the image conjured by the term "left-behinds", as if these implements of survival were left waiting for their owners to return for their use in afterlife. *Can't take it with you!*, she thought.

Maybe these tools were left behind because they were no longer needed, new tools having taken their place.

She sank into her sofa as the image connected with her personal reality. Was Middleboro perhaps awaiting hers and Taylor's return? The idea of replacing Mike was unimaginable.

In this immediate aftermath of the exhausting move to Raventon, and the continuing uncertainty with Mike, she pondered with a sense of devilish guilt the notion of how liberating it might feel to leave it *all* behind, to chuck *all* her possessions, *all* her responsibilities, and to start anew in her old, wooden cave. Simple as that.

Simplicity has a beauty - and an ugliness - all its own, she thought.

"Taylor would love to stumble upon some ancient artifacts, left-behinds. So, they're not trespassing, are they?"

"Not at all, ma'am. The State hasn't posted any similar signage, and they haven't blocked entry to the cave. If it was considered a hazard, they would have done so."

"What exactly does the state consider a cave hazard?"

"Holes, pits, drop-offs, flowing streams, unstable boulders, stuff like that. I visit the cave now and again just to make sure teens aren't using it for parties and that it's not being littered upon. As far as I know, the cave gets no recreational attention. Only reason Bobbi Leigh knows about the cave is because I blabbed about my left-behinds to her daddy."

"How deeply did you explore the cave, Sheriff?" asked Susan as she doodled an arrowhead in the margin of a sheet of paper.

"Deep enough to know it's not deep. There are a couple of very narrow passageways that I've not explored, but their openings are too small, even for the hopelessly curious, like me. I've positioned some boulders over these openings to discourage such attempts. Probably dead-ends anyway. The cave has one large room, extending about fifty feet straight inside the entrance. The ceiling there is covered with soot, apparently from ancient campfires. That room's where I found most of my left-behinds."

"Thank you, Sheriff. I appreciate your time. Maybe I'll ride over there."

"Feel free, Mrs. Smart. Want me to ride by just to make sure everything's okay?"

Susan considered the offer. "Like you said, Sheriff, I'm sure they're okay. I don't want to trouble you. Taylor doesn't appreciate a helicopter mom, especially while she's trying to establish her "cred" with friends in a new community. I've asked Taylor to be home by three o'clock. I'll let you know if I need your help. Thanks again, Sheriff Hagan. I do appreciate your reassurance."

"Anytime, Mrs. Smart. And it's no trouble at all. Have a great day."

Ever the writer and critical appraiser of phrases, Susan winced unforgiving at the hackneyed closing words from Sheriff Hagan as she ended the call. "Have a great day" sounded pretentious to Susan, the sort of banter used by bank tellers, salespersons, and grocery store clerks to dismiss their customers. Susan believed such phrases served as crutches of both the insincere and the pompous, though she dared not voice her bias aloud.

On the other hand, the Sheriff seemed nice enough, a sincere man. I'm sure he meant well.

She sighed and glanced at her watch. "Got to email my article to Home Manicure, *now!*"

Mark Randolph Watters

14

Chambers, Skulls, Bones and Theories

"Facts do not speak for themselves. They speak for or against competing theories."
- Thomas Sowell

"*Bones*, Bobbi Leigh!"

"I know; I *see* 'em!" Bobbi Leigh said as she surveyed the ghastly scene of scattered ribs and femurs, her flashlight illuminating the array from left to right. Bobbi Leigh scanned the area with her light, wondering what other horrors she might discover. "D-Don't look now, Tay, but check out the wall *beside* you."

Slowly, Taylor turned, interpreting the message in Bobbi Leigh's widened, focused eyes.

"Aaaah!"

Startled, Taylor took a quick step back, just as she might had she come face to face with a ghost, several ghosts, which wasn't that far from the truth.

Ten skulls, all human, lined a ledge side by side five feet above the cave floor. Their eyeless eyes stared straight into the girls' bulging ones. Clenched teeth almost rattled a percussive funeral air in silent, satisfying laughter at a macabre joke only skulls understand.

A shapeless pile of cream-white bones– femurs; tibias; fibulas; humerusi; phalanges; ribs and spines; clavicles; pelvises and more–covered the floor below the skulls.

The girls found no words and struggled to suppress soundless screams pressing against their throats.

"Look at *this!*" Taylor shouted finally, jerking her hand away from the boulder it propped against. She examined the boulder, forgetting momentarily the bony carpet. "Some kind of drawings, like *cartoons,* scratched on this rock!"

Bobbi Leigh shone her flashlight on the drawings and chuckled. "Petroglyphs," she said.

"Petroglyphs?"

"I thought you knew cave stuff."

"I know cave stuff well enough, thank you very much. I don't know petro-whatever stuff. I always called this sort of thing cave art."

"Or in this case, *cartoons!* They're called petroglyphs, Tay. Indian rock carvings."

Bobbi Leigh counted ten running stick-like figures under several zig-zagged lines, lightning bolts perhaps. Chasing the figures were swirly scratches.

"What are these?" Taylor asked regarding the swirly scratches.

"Wind, maybe? You know what? Look! Same number of skulls on that ledge as stick figures on this boulder, Tay. These bones must belong to these skulls, all of which go with these petroglyphs."

"You *think?*" Taylor said with ample sarcasm. "By the way, I know plenty about Indian rock carvings, but the only *petro* I've heard of has to do with oil! I *am* allowed a new word now and then!"

Taylor took seriously any suggestion her vocabulary lacked expertise beyond her years.

"So now you know a new word," Bobbi Leigh replied. "Happens to the best of us!"

Then, with a raised eyebrow, Taylor felt the smack of a recollection, a vague image of running stick figures, like the flash of a dream. Déjà vu, perhaps?

Where have I seen this before? Taylor thought.

"Think these skeletons are ancient, Bobbi Leigh? Native American, that is?"

"The Legend of Tucker's Mountain, Tay!" Bobbi Leigh whispered urgently. "Ten skulls. We've *found* those *ten kids!*"

"Oh, my *gosh!* What about the rock drawings? Who do you suppose did *those?*" Taylor asked.

Bobbi Leigh pondered.

"According to the legend, a *tornado* struck Raventon that afternoon. A tornado in the middle of *autumn!* That by itself is *whacko!* I mean, who ever heard of a *tornado* in the middle of *autumn!* Look at these wavy scratchings in the rock, like they were running away from something–a *tornado*–when they found this cave!

"The storm was probably too close to risk a run for home, so they ran inside the first cover they came across–this same cave–to get away from the storm."

"Obviously, they found the passageway to this chamber, too" Taylor said. "But why would they do *that?* It's so obscure, so *not* obvious. Besides, the entrance room is plenty large enough for shelter, even from tornadoes."

"Obscure *now*, maybe, but probably not so much then. Could have been larger passageways to this part of the cave then, openings that *are* obscure today.

"So they came back here, but they couldn't find their way out," Bobbi Leigh continued, circumventing Taylor's logical observation. "No flashlights, you know."

"But how would they have been able to scratch out these neat little stick drawings if they had no light?" Taylor asked.

"Good point, Tay."

Bobbi Leigh knew good points when she heard them, even if she were not so adept at making them.

The girls stared at the pile of bones and skulls and at each other for a couple of minutes.

"They were *brought* here, Tay ... *after* they were dead! Whoever dragged them into this part of the cave was not expecting their quick discovery. Not even Sheriff Hagan knows about the existence of these bones."

"How do you explain the drawings?"

"Don't you see, Tay? He–let's call him the *dragger*–made these drawings as a message to the eventual finder to say that these kids were caught by the storm, the tornado!"

"Maybe lightning killed them," Taylor suggested, "*before* they could get to the cave, hence the lightning bolt drawings, *that* sort of a message?"

"Could be. But why, then, would someone *leave* their bodies inside a cave, away from clear view? Why not just contact their families, have them come get their kids' bodies from the cave's entrance chamber?"

"No cell phones," Taylor replied.

"What?"

"No cell phones!"

"Funny."

"Well," Taylor speculated as she poked the pile of bones with her shoe, "maybe whoever found the bodies in the woods placed them inside the cave to protect them from the elements, scavengers ... you know ... wolvsies and bearsies."

"Wolvsies ... and *bearsies?*"

"Work with me here, Bobbi Leigh! The dragger, who might have been a Native American, hence the petroglyphs, couldn't transport ten dead kids back to town, especially not knowing where their families lived. For all the dragger knew, these kids weren't even from Raventon. So, he placed them here, out of sight and smell of whatever stalked these woods–wolves, bears, and such–until their families could be found. Decomposition must have done the rest, eventually."

"Decomposition?"

"Yes, *decomposition.* You know, *dust to dust!*

"I know what decomposition *means!*"

"Bodies *will* rot, you know!" Taylor exclaimed.

"Of course, Tay, but how's a cave going to *prevent* that? The dragger must have known the bodies would rot. Might as well have left them to the wolvsies and bearsies!"

"Exactly the opposite, Bobbi Leigh. He meant to preserve them as long as possible. While caves can't *prevent* decomposition, caves do have a near-constant 55-degree temperature, and farther inside, the air could be much drier and not as accessible by predators. Perfect for short-term preservation!

"The dragger—I *hate* that term; let's call him the *rescuer*. Much more noble-sounding, don't you think? Even if those kids were already dead, I think his intentions were good. The rescuer, unfortunately, was maybe killed by the storm, too, before he could contact the families in Raventon. Remember, folks had no early warning systems in those days, except what their eyes and ears told them ... that, and maybe a swelling of their knee joints.

"Maybe a falling tree killed him, or another storm, as he made his way to Raventon to tell someone. Either that, or he didn't want to face the very *real* possibility of anyone accusing *him* of murdering ten kids."

Bobbi Leigh moved her flashlight along the row of skulls, spreading the rise and fall of eerie, moving shadows.

"Those *poor* kids!" Bobbi Leigh observed.

Taylor sighed. "Anyway, this is where I'd want somebody to put *my* killed-from-a-storm body until my family could come get me."

"Stop it, Taylor! What if they *were* alive in the cave and died in here, *right here!*"

"Okay, okay! Let's say for the sake of argument they were *not* killed by lightning and that there was no benevolent rescuer trying to protect the bodies until their families were contacted."

"Benevolent? Where do you *get* these words?"

"I read a lot. The word means 'nice'. Now, let's say the kids found the cave for shelter, as they fled the storm, and even found the tiny passageway we just crawled through, convinced this was their only way to escape the storm's full wrath, given there *was* a tornado, legends being what they are. Hey, maybe they were already inside exploring this cave and were caught by the storm. They had somehow managed to make and carry a torch fire back into this area–"

"A *torch fire?*" Bobbi Leigh interrupted with doubt, challenging the details of Taylor's speculation.

Taylor ignored the interruption.

"–for warmth and light, which eventually died out in this room, probably as they finished scratching out these stick figures. For *fun*, for a *message*, I don't know. I'm just *saying!* It *could've* happened!"

"That is *so* random! How'd they make a *torch fire?* With matches? I know! They held a stick high over their heads and let lightning strike it!"

"Ha, ha. You're such a hoot! I don't *know*, Bobbi Leigh! Yes, *matches*, why not? Matches existed then."

"Somehow I can't picture 18th-century kids carrying boxes of Diamond matches."

"Okay, so maybe they had made the torch fire before venturing into the woods, who knows! Let me finish my slant on this thing, okay? Then you can shoot it down.

"Anyway, see how this tenth figure is not quite as straight as the others, not even finished? Maybe their fire flickered and died. They panicked inside this cave, lost, unable to find their way out of the pitch darkness," Taylor pondered. "They starved to death."

"Ye-e-e-a-a-ah," Bobbi Leigh said, stretching out the word as her eyes cocked upward, thinking just how frightening their ordeal must have been, regardless of the actual sequence of events. "It must have been blacker than death itself back here. Not even a *smidgeon* of light or the hope to ever again *see* light!

"From this spot, it would have been too dark for them to find their way to the tiny opening leading back to the room just inside the cave entrance, not to mention light enough to crawl through that long, curvy passageway. I mean, they didn't have one of *these* babies!" Bobbi Leigh nodded and tapped her SureShot Sentinel 250-lumen flashlight. "Probably banged their heads over and over, like mice in a maze, on stalactites and from falling over stalagmites. Must've been *panic city* in here!"

Taylor sensed Bobbi Leigh's skepticism. "Okay, then, what's *your* opinion?"

"Well, Tay, your opinion is as good as any, I suppose, but think about it. Who *stacked* their skulls on this ledge, in a neat row? Wolvsies and bearsies?" Bobbi Leigh giggled.

"Like I know the answer to that? Could've been cave explorers in subsequent generations; could've been Native Americans hiding out from the Trail of Tears."

"Subsequent?"

"Get a dictionary! Are you suggesting they died in another area of the cave, perhaps the front room, or maybe ... someone killed them *outside* the cave?" Taylor asked.

"That's exactly what I'm suggesting, Tay," Bobbi Leigh answered.

"So, you don't believe they died of exposure and starvation, lost in this cave, and you're thinking the storm *didn't* kill them. Then *what?* And there's still the nagging question of how their skulls ended up on this ledge."

"Not so much 'what', perhaps," Bobbi Leigh replied. "More like ... '*who*'".

"So we're back to wolvsies and bearsies?"

"Perhaps. Unless ..."

"Unless? Girl, you sure have a way of throwing a curveball! Unless *who?*"

"Unless ..." Bobbi Leigh said, staring intently into Taylor's eyes, urging her to connect the dots.

"The Raventon Witch!" Taylor said, stumbling over each improbable syllable as they dropped from her mouth.

"Bingo!" Bobbi Leigh shouted, delighted with the idea. "Let's look around for clues. Maybe something besides bones has survived these two hundred years."

"You don't really think ... *c'mon*, Bobbi Leigh, how could a *witch* be possible. You make it sound like *Hansel and Gretel*, for Pete's sake!"

The girls stood silently, contemplating the thought. Instantly, the cave felt sinister, darker. Boulders took on faces. Pulsating shadows looked other-worldly. Hansel and Gretel didn't seem so fairytale-ish after all. The familiar, monotonous sound of rushing cave air seemed to transform into the bellowed groans of trapped souls, they, too, unable to find their way out.

Taylor offered Bobbi Leigh a sandwich and water, which she took, and the two ate lunch while examining the silent expanses in search of clues in the chamber of skulls. Time slipped away in this timeless subterranean world.

"I heard noises last night, Bobbi Leigh," Taylor said, "creepy stuff, sort of like someone walking, make that *stalking*, across the upstairs floor, before you came over. Stuff was being moved around, sliding across the floor."

"Sliding? You *do* live in *one creepy house*, Tay. And your next-door neighbor doesn't help matters."

"Next-door neighbor? You mean Miss Peasy? She's harmless! Peculiar, yes, but harmless." Taylor said, eyes squinting at another of Bobbi Leigh's curveballs.

"Look, your house is heavy on the spooky side, right? Everybody knows it. Yeah, your Dad did wonders to that old place, but even *he* couldn't paint over its, shall we say, less-than-stellar history. Miss Peasy does nothing but bring attention to it, like a clown holding up a circus sign; she only *adds* to the general creepiness."

"Clowns *are* pretty creepy," Taylor admitted, conjuring some long-latent toddler memory.

"If you ask me, *yes!*"

"She's a pilot, Bobbi Leigh, and she owns an airplane. Takes something special at her age to do that. But, then, she *is* a bit creepy," Taylor agreed, eyebrows arched. "What 'less-than-stellar' history?"

"A *bit* creepy? She gives my *chill bumps* chills. If I had a dollar for every nightmare she's given to me, given to the whole *town*, I'd ... well, I'd have a *lot* of dollars," Bobbi Leigh said, scratching her head in search of words.

"You'd have a lot of *spent* dollars and a closet full of Red Motor jeans!" Taylor teased. "She's *that* bad, Bobbi Leigh? I admit she's goofy at times, downright strange even, but *nightmares*?"

"Some say *she's* the Witch," Bobbi Leigh revealed.

"Of Raventon?" Taylor finished.

"The very same, only two hundred years older."

"That's *impossible*, Bobbi Leigh."

Taylor laughed uncomfortably, knowing how ridiculous such a notion would sound *outside* the cave and in the protective light of day. But inside the nowhere-to-run darkness of the cave, confronted by skulls and bones, it sounded downright ... *right.*

"I know, but the legend *has had* new life lately, what with your ... dad missing." Bobbi Leigh briefly considered the possible insensitivity of her remark but quickly dismissed her guilt.

"*Police* think he's dead," Taylor added, dropping her eyes. "Mom and I ... we've adjusted."

"Precisely my point. The police here are clueless, have been from the start. Literally clueless. No witnesses, no DNA, no hair, no fibers, no blood, no-" Bobbi Leigh said as she peeled one finger after another, making her point.

"No *body.*"

"Sorry, Tay, I didn't mean ..."

"It's okay. Having not found Dad's body is a fact we're clinging to. It's our thread of hope. Anyway, you were saying?"

"And, living next door, she was probably the last person to see your dad; ever think of that?"

Taylor hadn't considered that possibility. And Miss Peasy had sort of revealed her jealousy of Dad's carpentry skills, Taylor remembered.

"But, they found his truck. Somebody else *had* to have seen him. She's harmless, Bobbi Leigh," Taylor said. "Disgusting and obnoxious, maybe. Different, yes; even good for a few laughs, but she's *harmless!* I mean, all she does is talk like the wind, smoke stinky pipes, and bake apple pies, quite *good* apple pies." Taylor smacked her lips.

"Maybe, Tay, but who knows what's *really* in those pies of hers!"

"Other than apples and sugar?"

"How about s*piders' legs* and *eyes of newts!*"

Bobbi Leigh paused to contemplate the culinary possibilities of *that* thought.

"She's always working on some sort of do-it-yourself project, if the junk on her porch is any measure! And at *her* age? Why doesn't she *hire* someone to do whatever it is she's doing? And I'm not buying the pilot and airplane ruse, not for a minute. A *broom*, maybe!"

Taylor chuckled. "She said she's as good a carpenter as my dad. I could have *slapped* her! Nobody's better than my dad, period! And then she spits this disgusting black gooey stuff, too," Taylor said.

"*As good?* She's comparing *her* skills to your dad's, after what he did with your house? That makes her nuttier than I thought. What disgusting black gooey stuff are you talking about?"

"Who knows! It's either licorice juice or maybe tobacco," Taylor suggested, wincing.

"Witch's chew," Bobbi Leigh offered.

"Witch's chew? What's that?"

"I just made it up. But, you've heard of witch's *brew*, right? Witch's *chew*! Get it?"

Taylor's face cringed and her lips curled at the mention of such an idea.

"I'd rather eat spiders'-legs-and-eye-of-newt apple pie! Let's look around for clues. What time is it?" Taylor asked.

Bobbi Leigh shone all 250 lumens of her overpowering SureShot flashlight square on the face of her round wristwatch.

"Two twenty. What time do you have to be home?"

"Three. And it took us over a half hour to get here. I need to leave by two thirty at the latest."

"Two forty. If you'd pedaled faster, we could have made it in fifteen," Bobbi Leigh said.

"Two forty then. My bike's a single speed. You have at least ten speeds and mountain-bike tires," Taylor pointed out, "not to mention mountain-bike legs. Your bike's perfect for hills and all the loose rocks and potholes. I need Miss Peasy and her *plane!*"

"*Clues*, Tay. Let's get to looking!"

"So you think Miss Peasy's the witch, do you?" Taylor probed.

"Next time you talk to her, Tay, look at her eyes. *Cat's* eyes! Green, slitted cat's eyes that never really seem to look directly at you. They seem to sort of stare slightly to your left, like she's talking to someone behind you. And her shriveled grin makes you feel like she knows something you *don't* know, like *you're* part of her secret."

Taylor let Bobbi Leigh's words sink in before changing the subject. "What're we looking for, Bobbi Leigh?"

"How should I know? But if you see it, let me know!"

Taylor and Bobbi Leigh scanned the floor of the cave around the bone pile hoping to find anything out of the ordinary, not that they hadn't found that already.

If indeed these were the bones of the ten missing kids from the great storm of 1795, the Legend of Tucker's Mountain, forever ensconced as victims of the Witch of Raventon, surely something else was here among the aged remains, something that might add credibility to an incredible tale. On hands and knees, they scoured, in search of the indescribable and the unknowable.

"Found an arrowhead!" Bobbi Leigh shouted.

"Really? Let me see."

Taylor Smart and the Chamber of Skulls

Bobbi Leigh handed Taylor a perfect triangular, stemmed point chipped from milky-white quartz, maybe three inches long.

"Wow!" Taylor said. "Anymore?"

"Maybe. This one looks *just like* an arrowhead Sheriff Hagan showed me a couple of months back. I remember it very well because it had the same tapered stem as this one and a light yellowing in the tip. Same size, too. Said he found it in the cave, like all his others. Must be two of 'em just alike."

Bobbi Leigh shrugged and pocketed the point. In the same moment, her SureShot flickered and dimmed.

"Um ... Houston, we have a problem! Taylor, get your flashlight!"

The words had barely left Bobbi Leigh's mouth when her light vanished, flicker and all. The girls stood awash in a depthless sphere of absolute darkness.

"Taylor, your flashlight!"

"I-I don't *have* it!" Taylor shouted, patting frantically her jacket pockets. "It must have fallen out of my pocket somewhere!"

Taylor swept her foot in a circular pattern, hoping to locate her flashlight, before disorientation overwhelmed her.

"So ... *this* is what blind feels like, what those *kids* felt like," Bobbi Leigh said, fear filling her mind like water in a doomed boat.

15

The Whispering Voice

"Whispering tongues can poison truth."

--- Samuel Taylor Coleridge

Susan finished the final edit to her Home Manicure article and read silently one last time, measuring the nuance of every word's intended effect. Leaning back in her chair, she took an insecure breath, and clicked 'send'. The text vanished, racing at near-light speed through the magic of fiber optics, just beating the two-thirty deadline. Relieved, she sank like a ragdoll into her chair, draping her forearm across her forehead.

"I am so tired," she whispered, followed by a wilting sigh. "Maybe some hot tea."

Susan sat still a few moments, eyes shut, as if hoping the tea would poof into existence on the silver serving tray of a hovering, white-gloved valet. She opened one eye, half expecting such. Another sigh gushed forth.

"Tea's *not* going to make itself, deary," she mumbled.

Finally, after a wrangling debate with reality, Susan relented and summoned strength enough to lift her inert body from the chair. Feeling a bit battered, like an athlete at the game's finish, she made her way to the kitchen.

Filling the teapot with water, Susan's eye caught the start-and-stop shuffling of the burlap-bagged Miss Peasy exiting her door leading to Susan's side yard. She ambled awkwardly, tapping her cane in one hand and balancing a steam-shrouded something in the other.

"Please," Susan whined, her cheek pressed against the door pane, "don't come over here. Not now."

Sure enough, Miss Peasy was coming over now, armed with a grin, a rounded cheek full of that gooey stuff, and another of her ridiculously tasty apple pies.

"Maybe if I just don't go to the door," Susan said, in her mind's haze forgetting she stood fully visible at the very door she hoped not to go to. She sluggishly considered her options, of which there really were none since Miss Peasy had already noticed Susan. "Fiddle, I might as well get this over with."

Miss Peasy made her way across the stone patio and, working her way around scattered chairs, rap-tap-tapped her cane on the kitchen door.

"Yoo-hoo!"

Susan smiled her freelance-writer smile, the same sort of smile she smiled when tolerating rejections from editors and their toothy words of 'have a great day' and similarly annoying faces and phrases. She opened the door.

"Hello, Miss-"

"Don't got time for tea now!" Miss Peasy squealed. "Just wanted to bring you this pie I pulled from the oven. Don't know how it got there. Just smelled something cooking, opened the oven, and there it was! Go on, now, take it and enjoy!"

Speechless, if for no other reason than the fear of being cut off mid-sentence, Susan took the pie and smiled. Miss Peasy noticed steam gushing upward from the boiling pot of water.

"Go on, now," she repeated. "Enjoy the pie with your tea. I got things that need tending to." And with that, Miss Peasy tapped away, a soft unrecognizable tune whistling from her lips. Staring, Susan held the pie until she realized with considerable discomfort she had no potholder between the pie and her palm.

"Ow," Susan said, blowing her fingers, as she turned to grab a hand towel hanging conveniently over the back of a kitchen chair.

"Pie's hot!" Miss Peasy said, back turned, but aware.

Susan leaned out the door and shouted back at Miss Peasy, in search of the appropriate words, "Thanks and, um, have a great day!"

Rolling her eyes and switching the pie to her other palm, she closed the door and glanced at the wall clock.

"Two forty. Taylor ought to be home in just a bit."

But Taylor wasn't home any minute, not within the range of "any minute" expected by her Mom. Susan stirred honey into her tea and took three rapid sips as she scooped a spoonful from Miss Peasy's scrumptious apple pie.

"How does she do it!" Susan marveled as she reveled in bite after bite of the divine wonder that was a Miss Peasy apple pie. Tea and pie consumed, she settled into the contour of her plush beanbag chair. Susan curled her legs to her chest and fell asleep. Three o'clock came and passed, then three fifteen, three thirty, four o'clock.

CR-R-R-E-E-E-A-K-K!! CR-R-R-E-E-E-E-A-K-K!!

Except Susan didn't hear it this time. The squeaky sounds from aged floorboards, and the strange taps that accompanied them, seemed to trek in a restless pace from one end of the upstairs to the other, stopping at times for a few minutes, and resuming.

"Ah, I see you're stirring a bit, waking up perhaps? Well, I've got something for that," the whispering voice said. "And, no, in case you're wondering, *no one* can hear us; I've been watching her, and she's sleeping, sound as a newborn."

The man with the whispering voice removed the cloth gag and lifted a water bottle to his captive's lips, tilting it, just enough to allow a trickle of liquid to flow.

"There now, you swallow. I bet you're quite thirsty. Nimrod! Go check on our ... guest. Tarry not, my friend! And make sure you're not seen!"

"I'm as stealthy as a midnight cat; don't you worry none about *that!*" Nimrod replied.

"Voice *down!* It's just that kid of hers," the whispering voice said. "Never know *when* that little girl's coming home, children these days!"

Mark Randolph Watters

16

Strength in Numbers

**"A faithful friend is a strong defense, and she that
hath found such a one hath found a treasure."**
- Ecclesiastes 6:14

"Ow! Watch where you're poking that hand
of yours!" Bobbi Leigh shouted.

"Like I can *see* where I'm poking?" Taylor
replied. "I'm just trying to find that passageway.
This *can't* be that difficult!

"Tell that to those ten skulls!" said Bobbi Leigh.

"Good thing we kept our bike helmets on. I keep banging into the walls and tripping over stalagmites," Taylor said. "Hey! What's this? I think I might have found my flashlight. Yes, here it is!"

Taylor clicked on the flashlight, its light also dimming.

"Make a mental note, Bobbi Leigh: get longer-lasting batteries for your ... um ... *Sure*Shot. There's our passageway! Let's get out of here. We've got to tell Sheriff Hagan what we've found."

"That's exactly what we *can't* do, Tay!" Bobbi Leigh said, grabbing Taylor's jacket sleeve.

"Why not?"

"What, and turn over our mystery to the police, just wash our hands of it and let them handle it, as if we never found this? Do you really want to do that *now?* Think about it. They'll rope off this whole area. The lake'll be overrun by reporters and newspaper people, then tons of archaeologists, not to mention the plain curious. You and me'll be nothing more than background noise. And when it's all over, tourists will know everything about this cave. We can kiss our little secret, *and* our cave, goodbye. We came up here to – ouch! Darn stalactite!"

"Told you they could be sharp!"

Bobbi Leigh rubbed her forehead and checked for blood. Finding none, she continued, "We came up here to explore a cave, and look what we found instead! This is *ours*, Tay! For now, anyway."

"I don't know, Bobbi Leigh ..."

"Look, it's not like the bones are new, right? It's not like there are any unsolved mur ... oops, I've done it again. What I meant was-"

"I know what you meant, Bobbi Leigh. Don't worry about it."

"Let's charge our batteries overnight and at least come back one more time, maybe tomorrow, and continue our search. Who knows what *else* we'll find!" Bobbi Leigh said.

"That's what worries me, that and this Witch of Raventon junk."

"I was just yanking your cord, Tay! You don't really believe that witch legend, do you?"

"So you're saying there's no legend after all? What about the bones, the drawings, the missing kids?"

"Sure, there's a legend, all right. Those bones, though, probably just the remains of prehistoric burials. You know, maybe a Native American campsite. I *did* find an arrowhead. And the Sheriff *has* collected tons of artifacts from this old cave. It's an archaeological gold mine, not the stuff of legends, okay! Hey, we ought to do a show for PBS and call it 'This Old Cave'!"

Bobbi Leigh laughed. Taylor joined in.

"True, you *did* find an arrowhead; that is, a *projectile point.*"

"What's the difference? And who cares!"

Taylor sighed.

"My Dad took me arrowhead hunting one time, down by some river, when a thunderstorm forced us to take cover under a huge oak tree, probably a half mile or so from the field and river bank. Not a smart thing to do, sheltering under a tree, but we did it anyway. After the rain and lightning stopped and the sun came out, that whole field took on a totally different look. I remember how excited he was as we approached that field, plowed up and all, rocks and flint sparkling in the sunlight like a pirate's treasure. I remember Dad's eyes sparkling, too. He said we'd find a lot of stuff out there, that this was the perfect spot for prehistoric habitats. He was right more times than not.

"A river ran by it, and we walked a little parallel ridge high enough to escape high water, had there been any. Perfect spot for a prehistoric habitat. I can still hear the sound, that gentle trickle of water over rocks. Turns out those rocks made up a fish weir.

"I remember picking up a shard of pottery wedged in a clump of hard mud. That shard had a complicated pattern of swirls and lines covering it.

I looked out across that broad field and suddenly I could visualize families of Native Americans carrying clay pots of water from the river; children scampering about, playing; groups of wattle-and-daub houses here and there, even a dog or three."

"Snap out of it, Tay!" Bobbi Leigh shouted with a clap of her hands. "Light's fading!"

"*Right!* Okay, we'll come back tomorrow. I want to find one of those, too," Taylor said, pointing to Bobbi Leigh's pocketed projectile point. "Wait a minute!"

"What now!"

"Mom and I are taking Miss Peasy to the airstrip tomorrow. She's going to show us her plane, and then, if Mom gives the okay, she's taking me up for a ride."

"Are you *kidding* me? You're actually going to let that crackpot take you up *there*," Bobbi Leigh said, pointing up. "Maybe it's not Miss Peasy who's the *nut!*"

"Mom's a pilot, too, Bobbi Leigh. If the slightest little thing doesn't meet her expectations, believe me, I ain't going *anywhere*. I've never flown before, so now's my chance!"

"It's your life. What time?"

"One o'clock. Shouldn't take more'n a couple of hours. After that, we'll come back here."

Bobbi Leigh added, "And after *that*, we'll tell Sheriff Hagan. Maybe."

A few minutes later the girls scampered out of the cave and into the wind of an approaching thunderstorm.

"Just as I feared," Bobbi Leigh said, scanning the sky. "Let's make tracks, Tay!"

Taylor checked her watch, suddenly remembering her curfew. *"Four-thirty already!"* she shouted. "I thought you said it was *two-twenty!* Mom's going to kill me!"

"Oops. Must have been ... four-ten? At least *your* Mom's home *to* kill you," Bobbi Leigh said.

Busy with her backpack, Taylor heard, but did not respond to, Bobbi Leigh's words of regret.

Thunder blasted.

"Let's roll, Bobbi Leigh!"

Mark Randolph Watters

The girls pedaled standing up, their weight rotating right to left to right in their efforts to outrace the storm. They rounded bend after windswept bend on their frantic pedal to Taylor's house. Leaves and twigs slashed the air around them, sometimes slapping their unprotected faces. They were slowed at times by a ferocious headwind, depending on the direction of the road's curve, but they managed to stay a bike's length or two ahead of the roiling storm. Egg-sized raindrops fell along the storm's leading edge, exploding in the road's dust around them like tiny water balloons.

Skidding into Taylor's driveway, the girls dropped their bikes and stepped the porch in two giant leaps, just beating the torrent (and a dangerously close bolt of lightning that split an elm tree across the street).

Unnoticed by the laughing girls as they out-quickened the storm, Nimrod watched from a living room window. Susan slept still, unstirred by the clamor of the encroaching weather. Surprised by the girls' swiftness from their bikes to the front door, he scurried from the room and up the stairs.

"Well? Is she ..."

"Still sleeping, yes."

"And the girl?"

"Coming inside, with a friend."

"A friend? Who?"

"That Harwell girl, Bobbi Leigh."

"Ah, yes, now I remember."

The wind pushed sheets of rain and missiles of hail against the house as thunder answered lightning in a frenzied conversation.

"I've got him back into a deep sleep. Ought to last through tomorrow morning, but we've got to move him! Can't leave him here."

"Move him *where?* And *when?*" asked Nimrod.

"Tonight, after the Smarts are asleep," answered the whispering voice. "I'll let you know where. Ready with the clues ... and the ghosts?"

"All set. Want me to paint more words on the walls, too?"

"Of course, but this time make it truly scary, not this namby-pamby "Boo" stuff, got it? I *want* this house, Nimrod, and I'm going to have it. The Smart family *owes* it to me, *Raventon* owes it to me, after what happened," the whispering voice said, fists and teeth clenched, his bloodshot eyes focused far away.

"But that was such a long time ago, and these Smarts–"

"And your point is? Yes, these Smarts had nothing to do with what happened then, of course, but the *point* is that the passage of time doesn't heal in this matter; it only *makes the wound fester!* What *matters* is this house and justice–*my* justice, *my* way." The whispering voice seethed, spitting his rage into the unconscious face of his captive. "And I shall *have* them *both.*"

Meanwhile ...

"Looks like Mom's asleep, Bobbi Leigh. Can you stay until she wakes up? There's strength in numbers!" Taylor said, scratching her tilted head and turning a request into a declaration of solidarity.

Bobbi Leigh opened her mouth to answer but was immediately distracted.

"Did you hear that, Tay?"

"Hear what?"

"Shhh," Bobbi Leigh urged, her hands outstretched and eyes looking up. Both were silent.

"What *is* it, Bobbi Leigh?" Taylor begged.

"I thought I heard a noise, the same kind of noise you said *you* heard," Bobbi Leigh replied. "Only ... now I don't hear it."

Thunder popped. Bobbi Leigh's eyes scanned other-worldly things that dominated Taylor's house. Ceilings as high as cave chambers; cream-colored notches of the dental molding; oversized chandeliers that looked more like inverted, crystal umbrellas.

Flashes of lightning punctuated her sense of uneasiness, surrounded by all the oldness. Her mind danced to the suggestive music of legends.

She recalled every climactic scene from every horror movie she had ever seen, all those dark hours spent alone with Ifs, Ands, and Buts. Her eyes began to form images of creatures that, if not real, appeared so.

"My head's gonna *explode*, Tay! If this house *isn't* haunted, it ought to be! All those bones and skulls we found today ... it's getting to me. I know it's just my imagination. Still ..."

"It's this *house*, Bobbi Leigh. There's something about it, something–"

"*Sinister*, sister! This house is a legend all its own! It's a regular death house, folks say!"

"A *death house*? Are you *crazy*?"

"Hollywood could make a blockbuster in this house, if some director had a mind to! Folks were *murdered* in this house, Tay! Facts speak for themselves, and no, I'm *not* crazy."

"Murdered? When?"

"A long time ago, of course," Bobbi Leigh answered with a shrug. "Any legend worth the label always happened 'a long time ago', but the way I heard it, five members of the same family were ..."

Bobbi Leigh cleared her throat. "Girl, it's too scary to *talk* about, even if it *is* just a legend!"

"Hey, don't quit on me now! Keep telling! Spill it, Bobbi Leigh! *Details!*"

Taylor could see her reflection in Bobbi Leigh's unblinking eyes. Something about this house, another of Raventon's raging legends, had Bobbi Leigh genuinely on edge, as if merely *thinking* about it might trigger a curse.

"Rain's letting up, Tay," Bobbi Leigh noted, craning her neck to peer out a window.

It wasn't.

"I really should be getting home. It's going on 5:30, and Dad should be home about now."

Susan yawned and stretched her arms. Glancing at her watch, she realized suddenly that she had slept nearly three hours.

"Taylor!"

"Right here, Mom."

Susan turned her head and saw the girls standing in the foyer. "When did you–"

"We've been here a while, Mom, at least since–"

"You still have your helmets on," Susan noted, unmoved by her daughter's dodge. "You two've been yakking in the foyer for *three hours*, forgetting to take off your … *wet* helmets? Try again."

The girls fidgeted for answers, shuffling their feet and exchanging guilty glances, searching for anything that might strongly resemble the truth, without revealing the *whole* truth.

"Um … we *heard* something, Mrs. Smart!" Bobbi Leigh blurted with hopes of diverting the conversation. "Upstairs!"

"Again? Look, girls, the house is old, more than a century and a half. Things are going to squeak and growl now and again."

"By *itself*, Mrs. Smart?"

"Depends on what you mean. Wood expands and contracts, a lot like Taylor's Dad during and after a big dinner. And, well, sounds happen."

Susan held her hand over her mouth and waited for the joke to sink in. Such excursions into humor helped Susan cope and cling to what little hope remained. The girls stared like scarecrows, not once realizing a joke had been made.

"Is your mom okay," whispered Bobbi Leigh, trying her best not to move her lips.

"She just woke up," Taylor whispered back.

Susan smiled and cleared her throat. "You girls want a snack, maybe some apple pie. Our favorite neighbor dropped one by earlier this afternoon."

Diversion successful!

"Ugh, I can't look at apple pie without thinking of Miss Peasy's teeth and chin," Taylor said, hand on belly. "How can such a filthy person own such a white bird?"

"She's not filthy, Taylor. Unkempt, maybe, but not filthy."

"Thanks, Mrs. Smart, but I do need to get home. Dad, you know. But, I'll see you tomorrow, Tay. Don't forget, *charge your batteries* overnight! And thanks for the pie offer, Mrs. S."

"I won't forget," Taylor answered. "You do yours, too! See you around 3:30. Are you coming here first?"

"Why don't I meet you at the airstrip at 1:00? I think I'll come watch. Miss Peasy, a *pilot!* This ought to be fun, assuming you *survive*, that is," Bobbi Leigh shouted as she deftly guided her bike through streams of runoff flowing briskly across the driveway.

Frogs croaked in hideaway places as the setting sun cut thin, yellowy strips of haze through the waning, spent storm clouds, throwing a surreal glow of amber and gold over the evening landscape.

"So, you two are going back to the cave tomorrow? Susan asked.

"After the plane ride, yes.

"Discover anything interesting in that cave?"

"The cave was pretty much empty, I guess; found a few flint chips, bats, stuff like that," Taylor answered. "I mean, a cave's a cave, right?"

Mark Randolph Watters

17

A Bar of Soap

"Necessity, who is the mother of invention."

- Plato

After a parmesan-coated spaghetti supper
and some mindless lounging in front of the
television, Susan and Taylor opted for an early
bedtime. Early, that is, until the knocking came at
the kitchen door, a startling series of urgent
thumps that released the adrenalin hounds and
set sleep back at least a few hours.

"Who in the *world* ...," wondered an annoyed
Susan, navigating the several right turns from the
living room to the kitchen. She needn't have

wondered at all, for she knew well the thumper. Susan sighed as she recognized the face squished against the glass.

"Coming, Miss Peasy," she said with soft frustration.

"Sorry to barge in on you like this, Mrs. Smart," Miss Peasy shouted, speaking twice as loud as was necessary and holding a half-eaten Zippy Burger in one hand, her cane in the other, and Percival peering unimpressed, "but I wondered if I might solicit your help, your daughter's, too!"

"What seems to be the problem, Miss Peasy?" Susan replied, grinning impatiently.

"Light bulb in the downstairs bathroom is blown. Now, normally I'd hop up on my ladder and change 'em in a jiffy, mind you, but this ... well, this ... you'll just have to see it for yourself. Oh, and tell Taylor to bring a bar of soap," Miss Peasy instructed as she turned and started for her house, cane tapping the patio stone.

"A bar of soap?" Susan whispered. "Doesn't she have her own?"

Rather than whip up any objections to Miss Peasy's inconvenient request, and further delay the inevitable, Susan shouted, "We'll be right over, Miss Peasy!"

"Don't forget the soap, deary! Need to add that to my grocery list."

Susan heard Miss Peasy's voice fade into a mish-mash of indecipherable mutterings. She shook her head, smiled, and closed the kitchen door.

"Taylor? Get a bar of soap!"

"Soap? What now?"

"Not sure, but grab a bar and follow me."

"Miss Peasy?"

"Miss Peasy."

"What's she up to this time?" Taylor asked, picking, then dropping, the slimy bar of just-used bathroom soap.

"Heaven only knows; something about her bathroom light bulb. Knowing her, this soap should clean up whatever the problem is."

"Good one, Mom! Maybe she intends to use it on herself."

"Taylor."

"Sorry, Mom."

Susan and Taylor left the house, soap bar in hand, on a rescue mission for Miss Peasy. Their departure did not slip unnoticed from the attic.

"Soap keeps slipping from my hand, Mom!" Taylor announced, frustrated.

"Wet soap'll do that, sweetie. Wrap both hands around it."

18

Buckeyes and Peppers

"There is no den in the wide world to hide a rogue."
- Emerson

"Nimrod!" said the whispering voice watching through an attic window. "The Smarts have left the house, gone to Miss Peasy's. Now's our chance!"

"Now?"

"Now! We've got to move our guest out of this house. We've been here too long as it is, and now that the Smarts are living here, we've got to relocate. And I know just where."

The whispering voice turned to his sleeping captive and smiled.

"*Move*, Nimrod! Take our guest to the car, the trunk! Don't forget to leave that snapshot of Mrs. Smart and Taylor in the attic, maybe under the words 'Get out'. Be sure to use that disgusting color of paint we took off Miss Peasy's porch. *And,* don't forget to spread a few of those Zippy Burger wrappers around. Leave those next to some chew splatter. Talk about *disgusting!* Collecting that germ-ridden junk was the worst part of all this. But, it *is* DNA, and that's the forensic key to *everything* these days. It places her at the scene, and it'll raise some eyebrows and cast plenty of suspicion, I'm guessing.

"Never did like that old woman anyhow," the whispering voice skulked. "Thinks she's better than anyone, the way she dangles that strand of buckeyes and peppers around her neck like some flashy costume jewelry! She *deserves* this fate. Pinning this on that witchy woman is as easy as two-for-one day at Zippy's.

"After all," the whispering voice said, smiling and keeping watch over Miss Peasy's house through one of Susan's attic windows, "she *is* the Witch of Raventon!"

"We gonna leave some haunting here tonight?" Nimrod asked, anxious to do so. "I like squeaking these old floors and painting stuff on the walls!"

"Won't need to. Opportunity knocks, and we have to take advantage. Let's go."

"Question?" Nimrod said.

"Ask it!" the whispering voice answered impatiently.

"You're rid of Mike Smart. You're directing suspicion to nutty old Miss Peasy. How does *that* get you this house?"

"It's *already* my house! It's sort of a legal thing; you wouldn't understand. But I've already found a buyer, an out-of-stater, who has offered me three times what Mike Smart paid for it. Smart was gracious enough to renovate the house for me, only he didn't know he was doing it for *me*. Now it's time for him to *step aside* so I can hurry along this little transaction of mine.

"We're talking over a *million dollars*, Nimrod! Once we've linked Miss Peasy to the disappearance of Mike Smart, Susan won't *want* to live here anymore. It'll then just be a matter of clearing some ownership hurdles."

"Are you saying Mike Smart ain't got clear title to this house?" asked Nimrod.

"Thanks to a close attorney friend of mine, no, he hasn't clear title ... or, rather, he *won't*."

The man with the whispering voice stared into space, his mind racing, ideas and thoughts ricocheting off each other like molecules inside a microwave oven.

"Couldn't you have cleared those same legal hurdles without going through Mike Smart to do it?" asked Nimrod. "And avoided all this trouble, to boot? I mean, what's he *done* to you?"

"If Mike Smart's so *smart*, he would have realized the legal flaws and made it right by *me* when he bought the house. Thing is, I believe he *did* realize the matter and *ignored* it. I won't make that mistake."

"So this is a *grudge* thing?" Nimrod pressed.

"I'm not telling you again to *get moving!* Those two will be back soon, unless, of course, Miss Witchy serves up another of her apple pies. You *do* want to be paid, do you not?"

"Miss Peasy's a pilot?" Nimrod asked.

"Yeah. What's *that* got to do with anything?"

"Nothing, I guess. Heard the girls talk about Miss Peasy giving one of them a plane ride, about the girls meeting at the airstrip tomorrow at 1:00."

"Plane ride? Hmm. Just got me a *fresh* idea. Let's move."

Mark Randolph Watters

19

Captive Transferred

An hour later, Nimrod and the man with the whispering voice slowed the car and turned at the muddy entrance to Lake Jasper.

Stuck between summer and winter, October in Raventon seemed obliged to the whim of uncertainty. Nighttime temperatures during this month spanned the range from a shirt-picking stickiness to the unforgiving shiver of frostbite. The sweep of cold air in the aftermath of the thunderstorm produced layers of ice over pothole puddles. These thin layers shattered underneath the tires, the crunch and splash breaking the frosty silence.

The mirror-still lake was empty of night fishers and way too cold for even the most daring of swimmers. Hikers would be out in droves as the day warmed, but not now.

Slowly, Nimrod steered the car past the cave, around a wind-downed pine tree blocking half the bend, and parked. Owls kept watch over the forest and lake, occasionally sweeping the air from branch to branch. Bats darted low as they executed absurd, supernatural maneuvers in their quests for insect bogies, like tiny fighter jets.

The pair dragged their bound, unconscious captive from the trunk and moved toward the cave's entrance, a leg or shoulder on occasion slipping from their grasp. Dawn's first light was just beyond those hills, maybe an hour away. The men donned headgear topped with lamps and entered the cave.

Inside, they tugged their captive across the floor and through icy puddles, with no regard for

what physical harm they might be causing.
Knobby stalagmites and loose boulders made the
trek rough, tearing clothes and bruising soft
tissue.

Nimrod crawled first through the narrow
passageway, the same route taken the day before
by Taylor and Bobbi Leigh. Hampered by extreme
spatial restrictions throughout the course of the
passageway, Nimrod and the whispering voice
finally managed to wriggle their captive into the
larger room, the chamber of skulls. Hands on
knees, the man with the whispering voice struggled
to regain his breath.

"Secure ... secure our guest here, Nimrod,"
he said. "The sedative should last until at least
noon. Be sure to roll the stones over the
passageway entrance when we leave. Can't risk
anyone hearing hollers for help."

"I'm curious ..."

"About *what*, Nimrod?"

"Why have you kept him alive so long? Why
not just ... you know ... and be *done* with it?"

The man with the whispering voice lowered his head shamefully, as if he were about to confess, of all things, a contorted sort of character flaw.

"I just haven't been able to bring myself to do it, that's why. I've been thinking about this problem for months. I knew I had to do something, so I got this idea yesterday for the cave. Hit me like a brick, the *obvious* solution! I should have thought of it *months* ago instead of keeping him doped up all this time. At least here, if he *is* found, it'll look like either a cave-exploration accident, or, as suspicion meets superstition, an act committed by the infamous Witch of Raventon, the whacky Miss Peasy."

"So that explains the leather necklace of dried peppers and whatever these brown things are," Nimrod observed. "Got this from her, didn't you?"

"Buckeyes, the brown things. She thinks they bring her luck and cure her headaches and such. Yeah, it's hers. Looks rather stylish hanging around that skull, don't you think?" the man with the whispering voice said, pointing.

"Downright *scary's* how I'd describe it," Nimrod muttered.

"It won't *bite* you!" the whispering voice said with a smile as he ran his fingers down the necklace. "It's *lucky!*"

"Speaking of scary, those *are* some pretty spooky bones and rock drawings in here. You do that, too?" asked Nimrod.

"I've had those bones for years. Dug 'em up in this very cave, in the entrance room. Native American burials, I'm guessing, from all the artifacts I found with them. As for the petroglyphs, yeah, those are mine. I wanted the message of the drawings and the skulls of ten persons to point to the Legend of Tucker's Mountain and to the lore of the Raventon Witch, who, as *everyone* believes, is ..."

"Miss Peasy! Native American burials?" Nimrod said, clearing his throat. "Ain't that, like, *illegal* or something, digging up those bones? Those burials are *sacred*, best left alone!"

"When the old house is sold, Nimrod, you'll get your cut. Don't forget that. You're not paid for your superstitions or your conscience. Remember this, too. I don't do 'legal' unless 'legal' helps *me!* Besides, these bones are still buried, technically. They're *underground*, aren't they!" the whispering voice said with a grin, pointing to the subterranean ceiling. "Now, let's get out of here while it's still dark."

"Let me just push this rock over the passageway hole," Nimrod said. "Thing's heavy! *Uhhnn!* How about some *help* here!"

"Not my job! What am I paying you for, anyhow!"

"My shoes slide on this wet floor. Can't get good traction."

"That's what happens when you wear *sandals!* Okay, *okay.* Hold on!"

"Watch out for the ..." Nimrod shouted, but it was too late. "... stalactite."

"Owww! Where did *that* come from!" the no-longer-whispering voice shouted as he slugged the stalactite with the palm of one hand while surveying the slice on his forehead with the other. Blood streamed down the slope of his nose and dripped to the cold floor of the cave. "Gimme a handkerchief!"

The whispering voice pressed the handkerchief against the wound, flexing and bending the fingers of the hand he used to slug the stalactite. Nimrod bit his tongue to suppress his laughter. The two exited the cave.

"What now, boss?" asked Nimrod.

"A cup of coffee and then we're going to pay a visit to the airstrip."

"The *airstrip?*" Nimrod thought for a moment. "Ah, I get it!"

"I knew even *you* would figure it out; you just surprised me how *quickly*," said the whispering voice.

Nimrod smiled. "Not as dense as you think, boss!"

"How's that old saying go ... luck is when opportunity meets preparation ... something like that. Anyway, the gods are smiling on us, my friend."

The man with the whispering voice wiped the bending trickle of blood from his forehead and brow and patted the painful injury.

"Dadburn stalactite! I thought I'd snapped all those things off." He shivered. "Brrr. Cold. Let's get that coffee!"

20

Just in Case ...

... know what I mean?

Sunday morning broke crystal blue and frosty cold, a refreshing crispness in the air. Leaves and branches, along with a few blown-over garbage cans, littered the ground. Weather forecasters predicted temperatures to warm into the lower sixties as this day progressed.

Susan poured bubbling water into her tea-bagged mug, wrapping her fingers around its rim and embracing the overdue arrival of her favorite season of the year. She sank into her kitchen chair and released a sleepy sigh as she scanned the newspaper headlines.

Rubbing the film of sleep from her eyes, a yawning Taylor shuffled across the kitchen floor to a waiting breakfast. She somehow avoided tripping headlong over a maze of half-empty boxes of utensils, cookware, and stacks of china.

"Morning, Mom," Taylor managed to utter, sweeping aside spikes and frizz of her still-sleeping hair.

"Morning yourself, sweetie. Hear any spooky noises during the night?"

"Slept like a stone, Mom. What's for breakfast?"

"Open your eyes and look," Susan said with a smile. "French toast and scrambled eggs, your favorites. You two going back to that cave again?"

"Yes, ma'am, this afternoon, after the plane ride. I'm taking my bike with me to the airstrip. Bobbi Leigh's meeting us there at one o'clock."

"Don't get your hopes up about any plane ride with Miss Peasy. It'll take more than a laminated license, a flight log of entries, and a pretty plane to convince me. She'll have to *demonstrate* her skills first, fly the plane solo. Did you charge your flashlight batteries?"

"I did, but I'm thinking of taking something more, maybe a few candles."

"Candles?" Susan asked with surprise. After a second thought, she added, "Maybe that's not such a bad idea, the luck you two're having with batteries."

"Some luck! It's a *just-in-case* thing, Mom. My batteries are fine, I'm sure, but you know what they say: can't be *too* careful. Bobbi Leigh found a perfect arrowhead in the cave yesterday. We're looking for more today."

"Sounds like fun. Sheriff Hagan mentioned to me all the "left-behinds" he had found in that cave. Bound to be more, I suppose. I'm going to the library this afternoon and do a bit of research on this house. I'm learning it has *quite* a history, and I want to try to confirm some of the things I'm being told. Want to join me this evening, before supper?"

"Mom, the *cave*, remember?" Taylor sipped her milk and wiped her mouth. "Besides, I don't want to do school stuff on a Sunday, not unless it's absolutely necessary."

"Ah, yes, now I remember. The self-imposed weekend library ban," Susan said with a chuckle. "You and libraries are like vampires and sunlight."

"Mom, you know that's not true. It's just that we'll be with Miss Peasy after lunch, whether we fly or not, and then the cave most of the afternoon, and well, if Raventon's library is like most others, they'll close at six anyway, probably five. Heck, it's probably not even *open* on Sundays!"

"It's open all right, until six. And it's not like this would be *school* stuff. But that's okay, sweetie; I completely understand. I've always admired your unquenchable quest for knowledge, be it in the classroom, the library, or the outdoors. You've always ...*spirited* me."

Taylor Smart and the Chamber of Skulls

Taylor sensed both the nibble of sarcasm and a hint of compliment. Not sure which was intended, she settled on "Thanks" and quietly focused on her French toast and scrambled eggs.

"I want to learn about the house's history, Mom, really I do," Taylor said, unable to let the matter go completely. "Did you put cheese in these eggs, extra-sharp cheddar?"

"I know you do, and yes, I did. Your taste buds are still asleep."

Taylor fidgeted the eggs with her fork. "More, please?"

"What, you storing up for winter?" Susan taunted.

"Funny, Mom. Hey, did you get your article for Home Manicure sent?" Taylor asked, shoveling a forkful of cheesy eggs into her mouth.

"Speaking of just-in-case, yes, just-in-*time!* Not sure how well it's written, but they'll let me know soon enough, no doubt. They always do."

"What was the topic?"

"Home repairs, of all things!"

"Did you mention Dad?"

Susan looked at Taylor and pulled her close.

"Dad'll always be the king of home repairs, Taylor. You really miss him. Me, too. You'll be happy to know I *did* mention your Dad. In fact, I devoted half the article to his carpentry prowess and to how he saved this old house."

"Thanks, Mom. Wow, it's eight already? I've got to take a shower and get ready for Miss Peasy!"

"I thought we weren't going to the airstrip until one."

"Exactly! No time to lose! And we can take sandwiches for lunch. Are my 511s washed?"

"No, but your Jeaniuses are, and-"

"Please, Mom, *not* the Jeaniuses," Taylor interrupted. "I'd rather wear dirty 511s any day, even to *school!*"

"Aren't they too big, even baggy? I don't think you have a belt that's tight enough. I'll have to add a notch or two."

Taylor propped her head in the palms of her hand and sighed. "Mom, don't you *know* that oversized is *very big* this year?" she quipped, followed by a wink.

Susan smiled and, muffling a sniffle from the range of Taylor's ear, she sipped her tea as she thought of the years of frightening exhilaration ahead. Not so much caves and plane rides, but adolescence, an unknown all its own.

Mark Randolph Watters

21

Go Fly a Kite!

"Kites rise highest against the wind – not with it. "

-- Winston Churchill

The ancient grandfather clock had no sooner bonged 12:30 when came the shrill known 'round Raventon, if not the world.

"Okay, y'all," cackled Miss Peasy, "let's go fly us a *kite!*"

"A *kite?* Mom, she's *lost* it ... again," Taylor whispered.

"In aviators' parlance, Taylor, a kite is a plane."

"Oh. Okay, then, let's go fly one!"

"Good afternoon, Miss Peasy," Susan said, trying to maintain a confident smile of greeting. "And how are you, Percival?"

Percival bobbed up and down a time or two.

"That's about all you'll get out of Perci, Mrs. Smart. Fact is, you're lucky to get *that.* He's taken a liking to you!"

"We're all set, Miss Peasy!" Taylor said. "Mind if I see that flight log one more time?"

"Not at all, Taylor. Here you go. Want to make sure, do you?"

"Not so much for *me*, Miss Peasy," Taylor answered as she tilted her head toward her mom.

"Oh, I see. Don't blame you," Miss Peasy said as she leaned over and whispered. "Never hurts to keep the evidence visible!"

"Shall we?" Susan asked, grabbing her van keys and motioning toward the front door.

"Readier'n a cow at milkin' time!" Miss Peasy answered, "and not *half* as jittery."

"Bobbi Leigh Harwell's going to meet us at the airstrip, Miss Peasy. Says she wants to watch."

"I s'pect after she sees you whirlygigging around in the wild blue yonder, she'll want a turn herself!"

Whirlygigging? thought Susan.

"Got us some Zippy burgers here, if y'all of a mind to eat on the way," Miss Peasy offered.

"I don't know if I should eat before going up, Miss Peasy. Don't want to *throw* up before we *go* up!"

"Nervous, child?"

"A tad. But excited, too!"

"It's all she's talked about, Miss Peasy. But there's one thing I insist upon."

"I know, I know, you want me to solo first, to show you what I've got, to see if I'm for real," Miss

Peasy said as she munched deep into a Zippy burger.

"That's right, I do," Susan confirmed. "You see, it's not so much that we don't *believe* in you; it's just that ... well ..."

"Seeing *is* believing, Mrs. Smart. Believe me, I get it. Don't worry yourself over it. I wouldn't let my *lunchbox* go up with someone I'd never seen fly a plane before. Take a right here, Mrs. Smart."

"Miss Peasy, now tell me again, how long have you been flying planes?" Susan asked.

"Includin' all the time *before* I earned my license?"

Susan's eyes widened. "Just ... just the licensed time will do."

Miss Peasy tipped her glance toward the sky, the sun accenting her emerald eyes, and gave a smile of reminiscence, as if a flood of memories had come cascading.

"Longer'n it takes hair to gray," she said softly. "Since World War II."

"World War II?"

Taylor Smart and the Chamber of Skulls

"When I was a child, Mrs. Smart, we were poor, *dirt* poor. Who *wasn't* in those days! And then along came the Depression, and well, we couldn't even afford *dirt*.

"My Daddy rode the rails looking for work, anything that might sustain us, anything that might drop another morsel or two on our plates or a penny in our jar. Sometimes he'd be gone for weeks at a stretch. I remember times wondering if I'd *ever* see my daddy again.

"At home, Mama rented space, for drifters. First the porch, then the parlor. Then, in the winter, when folks started demanding warm beds, she got to renting out *my* bed for a nickel a night. I slept on the floor, since I was the oldest and was better suited for such discomforts. My brothers and sisters got to sleep with Mama. Sometimes I slept on the dining room table, such as it was. Folks could find a free, cold floor or sidewalk just about anyplace, but a warm bed? That was special, and if they had it, they'd pay hard cash for the privilege.

"We got by on them nickels, and the quarters from a few odd jobs my daddy would sniff out. I made me a pledge then and there that I would make my parents proud of me, that I would make the very best of the opportunity they'd clawed and scratched to give me.

"So, when the time came, I joined the U.S. Army Air Force in 1942 as a test pilot, seeing it as an opportunity to better myself and learn new skills, many of such as were denied to women in those days."

Susan kept a razor-sharp focus on Miss Peasy's extraordinary revelation. Miss Peasy sighed and continued.

"Long story short, Mrs. Smart, I flew P-51 Mustangs, forty-two bomber escort missions, to be exact, over France and Germany in '44 and '45. Shot down eighteen Me-109s and a couple of Heinkle 111s. Impossible to believe, I know, but the stories I could tell you." Miss Peasy lowered her head, softly turning it side to side, and gave a slow sigh.

Susan sat, unable to form words. Then she revealed, "My father flew B-26 Marauders ...with P-51 escorts."

"Ah, the *Widowmaker*," Miss Peasy said, eyes closed. "Escorted those babies, too, and B-29 Superfortresses."

"Dad flew missions to knock out V-1 rocket launching sites in Germany. He spoke often of how P-51s kept him airborne; saved his skin, and his crew's, time after time. Could it be possible, Miss Peasy ...that *you* are the reason I ...and Taylor ...are ... are *here* today?"

"I knew there had to be a good reason for sleepin' on dining room tables!" Miss Peasy said with a wink and a grin.

Taylor's heart pounded faster with excitement.

"Is that your Cessna sitting out there next to that tree?" she asked, breaking her silence of awe and pointing to a white wing-over-body plane sparkling like a patch of snow in the midday sun.

"Mine, indeed! Had it pulled out of the hangar yesterday for some maintenance. Ought to be fit as a Stradivarius. Park right there, Mrs. Smart. Taylor ... let's go fly a kite!"

"A *kite?* But I thought ...oh, *yeah!* Never mind," Taylor said, remembering this piece of aviator's parlance.

The three exited Susan's Odyssey. Miss Peasy walked straight toward the plane, tapping her cane and whistling some out-of-time, out-of-tune tune. Taylor ambled several yards ahead, anxious to touch the glistening specimen of aircraft beauty.

"Go ahead, Taylor," Miss Peasy shouted with a point of her cane, "look her over! Flossy's as anxious as a chained-up dog!"

Unknown to the trio, in a car parked behind the cover of roadside kudzu, Nimrod and the man with the whispering voice watched the unfolding scenario.

"Yonder comes Bobbi Leigh!" shouted Taylor.

Bobbi Leigh raced across the flat field, sliding her twenty-one-speed mountain bike to a slanted stop just inches from Taylor.

"Afternoon, Bobbi Leigh! You wouldn't be trying to *kill* us, now, would you?" Taylor said with a laugh.

"Nah, just leave you wondering," Bobbi Leigh kidded. "Nice and cool this afternoon, perfect for constant-temperature caving ... and *flying*!

"Top of the evening to you, Bobbi Leigh Harwell," Miss Peasy said, who, on occasion, referred to any point past noon as evening.

"Evening to you, Miss Peasy. That *your* plane?" Bobbi Leigh replied with awe, having never adjusted to the majesty of seeing an actual plane up close. Then, turning to Taylor, she added, "I see you wore your necklace, Tay."

"It's *her* plane, Bobbi Leigh, okay? And what's wrong with wearing the necklace?"

"Nothing, of course, but *511s*, Tay?"

Taylor cupped the projectile points in her palm and looked toward the plane. "The necklace is ..."

"For luck?" Bobbi Leigh said, offering the words Taylor would not say.

"*No!* Not necessarily. I see *you're* wearing capris," Taylor replied. "Isn't that a bit cool for biking and caving and such?"

"*Very* cool! They're Red Motor."

"I meant *temperature*-cool, as in how they feel on your legs."

"Oh, yeah, maybe, but at least they don't snag on my chain sprockets. That can turn a really great bike ride sour in a *jiffy*. By the way, these Red Motors are *cropped*, not capri."

"Well, excuse me!" Taylor said, hands on hips in mock frustration. Taylor marveled with a smidge of envy just how fashionably-correct was Bobbi Leigh regarding personal apparel.

"511s are okay for biking, I guess," Bobbi Leigh noted, "*if* they're straight-legged. For my money, CHs are the way to go in straight-legs."

"Bobbi Leigh, if you'll look closely, I'm *not* riding my bike!" Taylor said.

"You did *bring* your bike, didn't you," Bobbi Leigh asked.

"Back of the van. Backpack, too."

CHs? Susan thought. "You're quite the jeans expert, Bobbi Leigh."

"Not really. I just like 'em. Hey Tay! Ready to rock?"

"Ready as can be, I guess. You here to fly with me or just watch?"

"Um, watch. Me and heights ...well, let's just say I'd rather look up than down."

"Afraid of falling, are you?" Taylor teased.

"Not so much the *fall* as the sudden change of direction. Anyway, got your batteries charged?"

"All charged. Yours?"

"One hundred percent!"

"Got your candles, Taylor?" Susan asked.

"Eight of 'em, in my backpack. Matches, too."

"Candles?" asked Bobbi Leigh.

"You sound like my mom. Just in case we have battery problems, not that *that'll* ever happen!" Taylor said, nudging Bobbi Leigh's arm.

"Good thinking! Okay, I'm ready to see y'all fly!" Bobbi Leigh unwrapped two balls of bubblegum, shoving both inside her cheek.

"Did you pack some sandwiches and water, Taylor?" Susan asked.

"Yes, ma'am, enough for both of us."

"Thanks, Tay!" Bobbi Leigh said, her eyes wide with relief, grateful *somebody* was not as single-minded as she. "I forgot all about food."

Taylor rolled her eyes. "No prob," she said. "You'd forget your *cropped jeans* if you didn't wear 'em to *bed* every night!"

"Funny."

"Plane's ready to roll, Mrs. Smart," Miss Peasy announced. "You all might want to stand over yonder while I crank 'er up."

'Crank 'er up' thought Taylor, sighing, feeling the breeze of freedom upon her cheeks and the

twinge of nerves in her stomach. She stroked her arrowhead necklace.

Susan, Taylor, and Bobbi Leigh retreated to the area in front of the van, perhaps a couple hundred feet from the plane. Miss Peasy, with Percival perched, entered the Cessna, and, after several minutes, started the engine. It purred. Taylor gasped. Susan placed her hands on Taylor's shoulders. Bobbi Leigh smacked her gum.

Mark Randolph Watters

22

Solo, But Not Alone

"She has not learned the lesson of life who does not every day surmount a fear."

- Emerson

"So, what was it you did to that plane, boss?" Nimrod asked between drags on his cigarette.

"Just a few minor adjustments, things Miss Peasy ... neglected to take care of. Seems her age just might be catching up with her, forgetfulness being what it is. And, seeing as how considerate I am, I wanted to be sure our friends experience the *full thrill and sensation* of fixed-wing flight."

The man with the whispering voice turned up his concoction of cola and peanuts and swallowed, his face cringing at the potency of the cola's carbonation. He stared across the field and sneered, satisfied with the self-perceived brilliance of his plan.

Miss Peasy angled the plane's path toward the grassy runway, shallow parallel ruts running its wavy length. The white Cessna rolled forward, its speed increasing.

"Boss," Nimrod noted, looking through his binoculars, "looks like Miss Peasy's the only person in the plane."

"I figured as much. Just watch, my friend, and be patient."

The Cessna picked up speed. Taylor tuned out all around her except the Peasy-piloted white plane as it lifted softly against an autumn blue background, its wings perfectly parallel to the horizon. Any doubts or disrespect she may have harbored for Miss Peasy Parlevous melted like snow in a fire.

Miss Peasy guided her plane to an altitude of several thousand feet, maintaining an oval flight pattern, until it looked no larger from the ground than a circling raven. At the peak of its height, she slowed the plane and tilted its wings side to side.

"Mom, what's happening!" Taylor shouted.

"Not to worry, Taylor. Miss Peasy's just wing-waving to us. Wave back!" Susan said, waving both arms in a wide sweep.

Miss Peasy regained speed and rolled the plane three times. Taylor and Bobbi Leigh gasped at the aerobatic sight.

"She's coming in!" Bobbi Leigh announced.

Miss Peasy's descent was postcard perfect. She touched the plane down as smoothly as if no physical difference existed between the ground and the air. She turned and guided the plane to a stop near the tree. After a few anxious moments, Miss Peasy popped open the door and exited with a cane assist.

"Well," she shrilled, "did I pass the audition?"

Taylor ran to Miss Peasy. "That was ... *perfect!*" she shouted.

"Thank you, Taylor. She's my *baby,*" Miss Peasy said, patting the Cessna's wing. "Ain't nothing about 'er I don't know, and sometimes I think there ain't nothing about me *she* don't know!" Miss Peasy laughed and tapped Taylor's shoe with her cane.

"So, Mom. What's the verdict?" Taylor asked anxiously in a full run toward Susan, as if she had to ask at all.

Susan thought for a moment. A woman who as a child gave up her bed for the good of the family and flew escort missions in World War II was worthy certainly of an ordinary writer's trust. More than a mere baker of apple pies and a master carpenter was piloting that plane! Much more. With a deep breath, Susan announced, *"Go for it!"*

Taylor and Bobbi Leigh shouted and, with the mighty slap of a high-five, leapt with joy. Taylor dashed back toward the plane.

"Tell you what, Taylor," Miss Peasy offered, "why don't we let Percival ride on *your* shoulder!"

Taylor stood statue-still as Miss Peasy made the transfer. Percival sat as comfortably atop Taylor's shoulder as if no change in perch were made.

"Off we go, Taylor," Miss Peasy said.

"Off we go, Miss Peasy!"

A light breeze swept across the open field. Bobbi Leigh and Susan stood side by side and watched the pair approach the plane. Despite all she now knew about Miss Peasy Parlevous, all the evidence that contradicted her initial impressions, Susan could not avoid the envelopment of emptiness she felt, knowing her Taylor was advancing beyond her reach, her help, her control. Or was she?

As suddenly as the propeller burst to life, sending leaves and dust in a swirly scatter, Susan broke into an abrupt run toward the plane, shouting, *"I'm going with you!"*

Miss Peasy smiled.

Taylor rolled her eyes. *Parents!*, she thought, repeating a Bobbi Leigh mantra.

Susan climbed into the Cessna and settled into the third of four seats, behind Taylor. Seatbelt fastened, Susan sighed.

"Ready!" she announced.

"Good to have another pilot aboard, Mrs. Smart."

"How did you know ... Mike told you, right?"

"That he did, ma'am. Now ... shall we?"

"Let's do it!" shouted Taylor, waving to Bobbi Leigh.

Bobbi Leigh returned the wave and shouted something inaudible to the Cessna trio. Taylor read her lips.

"Wheels wobbly," Taylor said, repeating Bobbi Leigh's unheard remark.

"Wheels *wobbly?*" Susan asked.

"Just the uneven turf and the runway ruts, Mrs. Smart," Miss Peasy assured the two, speaking loudly in competition with the drone of the plane's propeller. "This ain't like a smooth airport tarmac.

Not to worry, though. Gonna be a bit bumpy till we get 'er off the ground."

"Wow, she sure goes fast, Miss Peasy," Taylor said.

"Seems fast, but not so fast really."

Just as the Cessna began its ascent, all heard a loud snap and thump. Miss Peasy looked out the port side and saw the shattered parts of her plane's wheel assembly bouncing and breaking across the field below.

"That what you done to that plane, boss?" Nimrod asked, peering through binoculars and drawing intermittently on the stub of his cigarette.

"Oops," the whispering voice said with a lilt, "did *I* do that? Now we just watch that tin can do its thing."

Both laughed.

"Miss Peasy, what was *that?*" Taylor shouted.

"Just a minor inconvenience, is all."

"You call that a *minor* inconvenience? We've lost our wheels! What are you going to do, Miss

Peasy?" Susan asked, hysteria mounting in her tone.

"Been in this type of situation before, Mrs. Smart. These Cessnas glide like balsa wood. I'll just take 'er up and circle around. And then we'll belly-land. Simple as a Miss Peasy apple pie!"

"Belly-land!" Taylor gasped. "Cool!"

"But, how could this have happened, Miss Peasy?"

"Well, Mrs. Smart ... could be the bolts sheered. They'll do that, you know. Could be a stress fracture give way, caused by the bumpy runway. Maybe ... sabotage."

"Sabotage? Do you really think–?"

"Strange world we live in these days, Mrs. Smart."

"No argument there, Miss Peasy ... but a *belly-landing?"*

"If anyone has a better idea, I'm all ears! Okay, I'm taking her down," Miss Peasy alerted. "You're gonna feel a might harsh bump and bounce and then a really loud sliding and scraping noise, sort of like somebody's sandblasting your ears. Get ready!"

Susan and Taylor scrunched in their seats, readying for the impact. Percival sat impervious on Taylor's shoulder. Miss Peasy held the throttle and wheel, her arms extended and the plane's nose angled upward.

SCREEEESSSHHHHH!

The Cessna sandblasted along the grass. Taylor and Susan screamed, grabbing the edges of their seats. Percival flapped his wings once. Miss Peasy held her breath. Nimrod and the man with the whispering voice stared in disbelief.

SCREEEESSSHHHHH!

Miss Peasy's plane bounced and skidded like a Zippy burger wrapper across Susan's lawn. It maintained its upright, nose-up position, but lots of skidding and breath-holding remained.

Mark Randolph Watters

23

A Flossy Belly-Flop

"Ya gotta do what ya gotta do!"

-- you, me, and everybody else

An infinity of minutes passed.

"Tell me when it's over!" Taylor shouted.

Finally, with the right wing gently tapping the turf, the Cessna's skid slowed to a halt. Miss Peasy sniffed the air for signs of fuel leakage. Taylor released her breath and opened one eye at a time. Percival scratched his head. The "strange world" had righted itself, if only for the moment.

Silence surrounded the plane and its occupants like an intermission, the music of passing flocks of birds the interlude. Miss Peasy issued a hearty cackle of a laugh.

"We're *alive*, Mom!" Taylor shouted, clutching her projectile point necklace.

"Of *course* you're alive, child!" Miss Peasy said, laughing.

Susan sighed and hugged Taylor.

"Miss Peasy, you did it!"

"I know, I know! I saved the propeller! Ain't it great! Not *one* scratch or dent on it! Ain't *never* belly-flopped before without wrecking the propeller! Those things are *expensive!*"

*You've done this **before**?* Susan thought. She smiled and with a slight chuckle, said, "Yes, well, that *is* great! But you saved *us*, too!"

"Oh, that. Weren't *never* in doubt, Mrs. Smart. We're as snug as corn on the cob and safer'n a baby in a crib. You see, the trick to these types of landings is ..."

"Y'all okay?!" screamed a sprinting Bobbi Leigh.

Doors opened on the plane and out stepped its pilot and two passengers, three if one counted Percival, smiles plastered ear to ear on each, except for Percival.

"Now, *that's* what I call a *plane ride!*" Taylor shouted, brushing the wrinkles from her jeans.

"That's what *I* call *divine intervention!*" Susan countered, as Miss Peasy stroked Percival's feathers. "And some dandy flying, too!" she added with a grateful smile.

"Your wheels just *dropped off*, Miss Peasy! You weren't twenty feet off the ground," Bobbi Leigh motioned with her hand and a whistle, "when the wheels dropped like somebody was holding on to them and just let 'em go!"

Miss Peasy scrunched her eyebrows.

"Hmmm. Sabotage, all right, Mrs. Smart. Somebody's been tinkering with Flossy here."

"Flossy?" Taylor interrupted.

"Whiter'n a flossed tooth, don't you think?" Miss Peasy answered. "'Cept for them green grass stains. I call 'er Flossy."

"But you have 'Amelia 45F' painted on the side!" Bobbi Leigh observed.

"That's her technical name. See, I always did admire Amelia Earhart. But, between me, you, and the plane ... it's Flossy."

"What's Amelia Earhart got to do with it?"

"I'm guessing that's where the '45F' comes in," Taylor observed.

"Very perceptive, Taylor Smart! That's how old Amelia would have been when she was declared dead. And, of course, she was a female, the 'F', you know. 45F!"

Taylor looked at Susan, both thinking of Mike.

"Um, Miss Peasy," Taylor said, hesitant to correct a person seventy-seven years her senior. "I think Amelia Earhart was forty-one when she was declared ... dead."

"Forty-*one*, you say?" Miss Peasy removed her baseball cap and scratched her frizzed hair. She studied a moment. "Are you *sure* about that?"

"I wrote a report in fifth grade about Amelia Earhart. They officially declared her "dead" on January 5, 1939, about a year and a half after she became missing."

"Forty-one. You don't say!" Miss Peasy said, wondering how a 'one' could have been mistaken for a 'five' on her Flossy. "Must be one of them – what do you call it? Typos? Shaw, I reckon I'll just have to make some changes to Flossy besides new wheels. Easier than changing the history books."

"So you believe your plane was tampered with, Miss Peasy?" Susan asked. "Who would do such a thing? Who would try to ... kill you?"

"Don't know if I was the *only* target, Mrs. Smart. Could be, mind you. But folks have had plenty of chances to do this sort of thing before. I always fly alone. So, why wait until I'm taking up passengers, unless ...? Something don't smell right, Mrs. Smart."

"Mom, Bobbi Leigh and I are heading over to the cave for a little while."

"Home before dark, young lady," Susan answered with a quick dismissal. "Should we go to the Sheriff about this, Miss Peasy?"

"Not yet. I want to check out what's left of those wheels and mounting assembly first. I need to rule out an accident or poor maintenance."

Meanwhile ...

"What do you reckon went wrong, Boss," Nimrod asked.

"Miss *Peasy*, that's what!" the man with the whispering voice answered, holding a blood-reddened handkerchief against the cut on his forehead.

24

Sudden Display of Defiance

"There is no week nor day nor hour when tyranny may not enter upon this country, if the people lose their roughness and spirit of defiance."

- Walt Whitman

"Did you tell your mom what we found, Tay?"

"Are you *kidding* me?" Taylor answered, adjusting her helmet strap. "And aren't you *ever* going to call me Muley?"

"Can't get used to it, Tay!"

"Anyway, it's *our* secret, right? And if I *had* told her, Mom wouldn't have let me come back. Did you tell your dad?"

"Nah, for the same reasons," Bobbi Leigh answered, mounting her bike. "But, then, my Dad couldn't care less whether I go back to the cave or not, bones or no bones. He's too busy paying attention to his *la-dee-da* clients to pay attention to me."

Bobbi Leigh paused, head down.

"Always told me he'd take me to the mounds, the museum, a ballgame, a concert or two, maybe even walk some fields around here and pick up some rocks and junk. Never did. I'd be happy if he just said 'hello' now and then." Bobbi Leigh shrugged. "Oh, well, whataya gonna do?"

Heading out for the cave, the girls skillfully steered their bikes clear of scores of beckoning holes filled with storm water, bountiful opportunities for the sport of splattering anything within range. They aimed instead for the unthawed craters lining the dirt road's shaded edge. Those they gunned for at top speed, crashing through the slush as they swung their legs up ninety degrees from the pedals, splattering themselves amid howls of laughter.

As they approached the big cedar tree landmark at Lake Jasper, after which the cave was located, they stopped at the side of the road to allow a car to pass. Bobbi Leigh recognized the passenger but not the driver. The car slowed and stopped alongside to the girls.

"Hi, Sheriff Hagan!" Bobbi Leigh said. "Some *rain* last night!"

"Afternoon, Bobbi Leigh. What're you two doing out by the lake on this chilly Sunday afternoon. Ain't you got homework? And why are you wet? Don't tell me you've been back to that old cave today!"

"Running puddles, Sheriff," Bobbi Leigh answered.

"So I see. Well, y'all aren't *intending* to go back to that cave, are you?" Sheriff Hagan asked, folding a splotchy red cloth and shoving it into his shirt pocket.

"Thought we might," Bobbi Leigh answered, her eyes squarely on the Sheriff's injury. "Um, any reason *not* to, Sheriff? Got flashlights; food – thanks to Taylor here – and helmets; water. Hoping we might find us some artifacts."

Sheriff Hagan turned his head for a look back and then glanced over to his driver, who kept his hands stiff on the wheel and his gaze forward arrow-straight, clouds of cigarette smoke curling from his nose.

"Well, Bobbi Leigh," Sheriff Hagan said, clearing his throat, "y'all got wetsuits? It's like this, see. Cave's pretty much flooded. We've just come from checking it out. Runoff from the storm has filled the underground stream, and well, it's just not *safe* in there. I'm afraid you'll have to spend your Sunday, probably the rest of your life, doing something besides caving in *that* old cave. In fact, it's pretty much been decided to permanently seal that cave, which we will likely do tomorrow. Who's your friend?"

"This is Taylor Smart. She and her mom just moved to Raventon, into that old spooky Hatcher house her dad fixed up before he ... oops, I did it again. Sorry, Tay."

"Bobbi Leigh, I told you, don't *worry* about it. Nice to meet you, Sheriff Hagan," Taylor said.

Sheriff Hagan peered at the afternoon sky, pretending not to notice Taylor's extended hand.

"There's a stream in that cave?" Bobbi Leigh asked.

Hagan ignored the question.

"Well–Ow!–you girls stay *out* of that cave, you hear me? And be careful on this road. I know it's Sunday, not much traffic, but you never know when some ... crazy driver's gonna round one of these bends and ... well, I think you know what I'm talking about. There are people not yet born whose accidents I'll have to work and whose funerals I'll have to attend, and all because of reckless drivers on this road and careless kids on their bikes."

Without so much as a *vibration* of their heads, Bobbi Leigh and Taylor shifted their uncomfortable eyes in a peripheral glance at each other. Talk about *left field!* The girls hadn't expected such an icy how-do-you-do lecture from the Sheriff.

Not only that, the girls could not help but wonder what had happened to Hagan's head. Taylor fought back a powerful urge to ask the Sheriff how he had received his injury but figured it must have been cave-related.

"Yes sir," they replied in unison.

"Tell Mrs. Smart 'hello' for me, Taylor," the Sheriff added as the car pulled away. "I'll be in touch."

"You think they got the message?" Nimrod asked as the car slowly splashed through mud and water.

"Maybe," said Sheriff Hagan. "Yeah, I think so. Doesn't really matter though. I'll go back in an hour and check on 'em. If they're in that cave–and I suspect they just might be–they're ...well, just an *accident* waiting to happen, I'm afraid. The plane was an unfortunate happenstance. It won't happen again."

Nimrod stiffened his left arm, his white-knuckled hand gripping the steering wheel like a vise. His thoughts shifted to the shrinking likelihood of collecting his share of the million dollars promised him by Hagan.

The girls mounted their bikes and slowly made their way opposite the direction of the cave, so as not to arouse suspicion, all the while watching as the Sheriff's car disappeared around the bend.

They listened for several minutes to the receding sounds of splashing water and the crunching of storm-felled branches as the Sheriff and Nimrod made their way along the curved shoreline of Jasper Lake.

Then, silence filled the air.

"We're going *back*," Taylor announced, "and we're going *in!*"

"Going *in?*" Bobbi Leigh asked, surprised at Taylor's sudden display of defiance. "What if he comes back?"

"He probably *will*, but we can hide our bikes behind some shrubs and vines. If he doesn't see the bikes, he'll think we're not here."

"I don't know, Tay. I mean, bike tracks and all–"

"There are bike tracks all *over* the place! Look, I want to check the cave for clues, anything that might tell us more about those skulls and bones. I saw something really *eerie* last night, Bobbi Leigh."

"Tell me."

"It was late, and Mom and I were getting ready for bed, when Miss Peasy rapped on the kitchen door."

"Cane?"

"Yes. How'd you guess?"

"Carries it everywhere she goes. Have you noticed the carvings of forest animals on that cane? Bats, owls, crows, even snakes. Not a

single deer or bear. Just the Halloween critters.
Weird!"

"It's normal for her. She wears buckeyes
and peppers on a leather necklace, too. But you
saw what she did today. Glided her plane down
like "Sully" Sullenberger. Saved our *lives!* She's
hard to figure, sometimes. Anyway, she wanted us
to help her change a light bulb stuck in her
bathroom light."

"*Who?*" Bobbi Leigh asked, unfamiliar with
the name.

"Who who?" Taylor replied.

"What are you, an *owl?* That *Sully* fellow."

"Captain "Sully" Sullenberger, the U.S.
Airways pilot that belly-landed that huge
passenger jet into the Hudson River a few years
back! Everyone survived. Don't tell me you didn't
know about *that!*"

"I did, I *do*; I just forgot, is all. How did her
light bulb get stuck, anyway?"

"The glass part had broken off, leaving only the metal base. I brought along a bar of soap. Didn't know why at first, until Miss Peasy–"

"Hey, how many witches does it take to change a light bulb?" Bobbi Leigh blurted.

"What? Why'd you interrupt me?" Taylor asked, annoyed. She sighed. "Okay, I don't know ... um, how many?"

"*None!* They just twitch their noses and the bulbs change themselves!"

Taylor stared unimpressed at a giggling Bobbi Leigh. "Have you no respect? Anyway, it takes *one* witch to twitch!"

"I'm teasing, Tay! *Lighten up*, so to speak."

Taylor sighed. "Anyway, after I climbed a ladder to reach the bulb, Miss Peasy told me to push the soap bar into the metal base of the bulb and twist. Voila! Bulb twisted right out. She's actually pretty good with solving problems, Bobbi Leigh."

"She probably cast some *spell* on the soap. Okay, so what was the eerie part?"

"Well, she offered us some pie–"

"Let me guess, *apple!*"

"She offered us some pie, and that's when it *dawned* on me!"

"*What* dawned on you?"

"Her *cap*, that silly baseball cap she wears!"

"What was so *eerie* about a baseball cap? Other than the fact she *wears* one, probably even to bed. And it makes her hair stick out like a tangle of Spanish moss!"

"Nothing eerie about the cap itself, just the stitching on the front of the cap.

"Stitching?"

"She probably bought the cap at a museum gift shop, but it was a scene of ten petroglyph-like stick figures running *after* something or *away* from something, very much like the petroglyphs in the cave, in fact *uncannily* like them."

"*Uncannily?* I know, I know, I'll look it up," Bobbi Leigh said.

"Really made me wonder about this Witch of Raventon stuff and a possible Miss Peasy connection. Unlikely, I know, but that's why we *have* got to go back into that cave, Bobbi Leigh!"

"I'm surprised at you, Tay! I didn't think you were buying any of that folklore junk."

"I'm not, I suppose," Taylor replied unconvincingly.

Bobbi Leigh flashed a smirk of doubt.

"I'm *not!* I really just want to see if I can find an arrowhead in there, like *you* did. So, let's *go!*"

"Maybe we ought *not* go in there, Tay," Bobbi Leigh said, reaching for Taylor's arm. "What I mean is … um, there's *truth* in every legend, right? Why take chances on which part–or parts–of the Raventon Witch legend … *might* be true? Besides, if that stream *is* up, and if there *is* floodwater in the cave, then–"

"Fine. *Stay* here. I'm gonna do me some *sleuthing!* At least be my lookout. Hide in the kudzu. Whistle, shout, sing, fart, *whatever,* just let me know if you see the Sheriff coming back this way. That way I'll know to kill my light and skedaddle behind some flowstone. While you're at it, cover over the fresh bike tracks if it'll make you feel better. Just make yourself useful."

Taylor stood staring laser-like into Bobbi Leigh's baby-blue eyes, determined to carry on. Bobbi Leigh realized Taylor's resolve as well as the futility of convincing her otherwise. Besides, she did not want to abandon her new friend and end up alone herself.

"Never mind, Tay. I'm going with you. You sure can be a *stubborn* one when you get your mind set on something, like a ..."

"A *mule?* Oh, and you're *not?*" Taylor said.

Both laughed in agreement, punctuating the response Taylor had hoped from Bobbi Leigh Harwell.

Mark Randolph Watters

25

The Discovery

"A discovery is said to be an accident meeting a prepared mind."

– Albert Szent-Gyorgyi

The girls pedaled the half mile to the cave and placed their mud-splattered bikes behind a thicket of rhododendron and wisteria on the adjacent slope.

"Flashlight?" Taylor asked, quickly confirming equipment.

"Check," Bobbi Leigh answered. "New batteries, too."

Taylor continued.

"Sandwiches. Check. Water. Check. Candles. Check. Matches. Check. Spunk."

"And how! Check!" Bobbi Leigh answered. "All set! Glad you thought of the sandwiches and water. Candles, too! What *are* you, a *Girl Scout* or something?"

"Troop 727, Middleboro," Taylor replied with pride.

Both tapped their heads with their palms to confirm the presence of helmets. Bobbi Leigh turned up the collar on her fur-lined denim jacket to keep her neck chills in check.

Indeed, unable to absorb fully the volume of water from yesterday's storm, the second in as many days, the ground at the cave's entranceway squished under the meager protection of their tennis shoes, soupy water sloshing above the shoe line and seeping into their socks, hinting at what the girls might encounter inside.

"Brrr! Sheriff Hagan was *right!* We *do* need wet suits! Now I know how deer feel!" Bobbi Leigh said.

Taylor Smart and the Chamber of Skulls

"Deer have *hooves* … and fur. Besides, they *love* this sort of thing," Taylor said.

"Oh, so you and deer are like *this*, huh?" Bobbi Leigh asked playfully, her index and middle fingers crossed.

"Ha Ha," Taylor mocked. "We have deer in Middleboro, too. Let's go."

Taylor thought it strange that the cave yesterday showed no signs of flooding as a result of Friday night's thunderstorm, a frog-choker by any measure. The immediate room beyond the entranceway, while damp and drippy, had drained well to areas unseen and had not flooded, not to any extent that pointed to imminent danger. The deeper the two ventured into the cave, the less slippery were the rocks and the less evidence that they would encounter worse.

Both wondered why the Sheriff so adamantly had forbidden the girls' passage into the cave. Maybe back-to-back storms had a history of flooding the cave eventually, nature's delayed reaction, as runoff eventually overwhelmed the underground streams.

Maybe the Sheriff spoke from his wealth of experience, Taylor wondered, considering the injury he had suffered apparently while in the cave. Maybe he was giving the girls the benefit of his fore(head)knowledge. Whatever the Sheriff's reasons, the girls defied them all. Such happens when friends peer at the world from the brink of adolescence and there's *sleuthing* to be done!

"Somebody's shifted this big rock over the passageway, Tay! Looks pretty heavy. How are we going to move it?"

"Check *this* out, Bobbi Leigh. No *flood* perhaps, but this cave *is* getting creepier by the day! First bones; now this. *Blood!*"

"Blood? Are you sure? Show me!"

"Right here," Taylor said, pointing to the floor, "several drops, redder'n scarlet satin; and it looks fresh."

Bobbi Leigh smeared a drop with her shoe. "Yuck! I think I'm going to hurl. Who do you suppose–"

"The Sheriff's," Taylor answered before the question was fully asked, "and don't you hurl, girl! He and that other fellow – by the way, who *was* that other fellow? – must have been inside the cave checking for flooding, like he said."

"Didn't recognize him," Bobbi Leigh replied. "He looked mean, like he didn't care a *frog's hair* for kids."

"Or anyone!"

"That cigarette he had in his mouth pretty much grossed me out."

"Help me move this rock, Bobbi Leigh. We'll have to get on our knees and *push* this sucker."

"On our *knees?* Can't we get some *deer* to help us, or maybe some ... *bearsies?* I bet if Miss Peasy were here, she'd just command it to move, and move, it would!"

The girls found the least wet spot to plant their knees and began their push. Water soaked their jeans at the knees and beyond, despite all, as their pushing intensified.

"My Red Motors!"

"Why'd you wear your capris to go *caving*, Bobbi Leigh? This isn't the *mall*, you know!" Taylor snickered. "Don't worry, they'll dry!"

"I know, I know, but for the last time, they're *not* capris; they're *cropped!*"

"Capris, ca-cropped, what's the diff?"

"If you have to ask ...*hey*, the rock, it's *moving!*"

"Just ... a little ... more ... There!" Taylor said between gulps of air.

"Flashlights!" Bobbi Leigh exclaimed.

The two crawled through the narrow, low passageway, soaking their jeans and skin from tummy to toe. The rush of air through the tunnel brought intermittent smells of dampness and flora, the former expected, the latter not. Inside the large room, the girls searched for the wall opening that led to the chamber of skulls.

"Where *is* it, Tay?"

"I thought it was–yes, *right here!* There's a rock in front of *it*, too! What *gives?*"

"It's even bigger. This wasn't here yesterday, Tay. Think we can move it?"

"Only one way to find out."

Back on their knees, the girls found cupped places on the boulder in which to anchor the curves of their shoulders. Deep breathes taken, they began the mighty push.

"Not moving, Tay! Shoes keep slipping."

"Mine, too. It'll move. Keep pushing, *harder!*"

After several attempts, they managed to tip the rock onto its rocking-chair curved side, which caused it to sway and roll away just enough from the passage for them to squeeze through the space.

"Man, we're good!" Bobbi Leigh shouted.

"Not so loud. The Sheriff might have returned, to check on us, remember!"

"You think he'd *really* do that?"

"There's something about him, Bobbi Leigh. I don't think I trust him, especially his driver."

Bobbi Leigh thought for a moment. "He never shook your hand, did he?"

"Not just *that*. The cave's not flooded at *all*," Taylor said, "not even *close*. I see no sign it might flood later from runoff unless the dam breaks, which it *won't*. Why would he act like we were in any for-real danger if we went inside?"

"Grown-up being a grown-up, I reckon. Maybe he figured that if *he* could smack his noggin, imagine what two little *girls* might do! Hey, what was *that!*" Bobbi Leigh said as she grasped Taylor's arm.

"I heard it, too. Sounded like a voice," Taylor whispered. "There it is again; it *is* a voice, *voices*."

"The Sheriff's?"

"Came from that direction," Taylor replied, pointing to the narrow passageway through which they had just crawled.

"I don't like it, Tay!" Bobbi Leigh whispered. "Not one little bit!"

"You think *I* like this?"

"This was *your* idea!"

"Come on, Bobbi Leigh, let's at least peek down the passageway and-"

"Taylor, wait! *Look!*"

Taylor obliged and turned, looking toward the floor where Bobbi Leigh shone her flashlight.

"That a *wallet?*" Bobbi Leigh asked.

"Looks *like!*" Taylor answered as she bent to pick it up. "It sure isn't any *prehistoric* left-behind."

Impatiently, Bobbi Leigh spurted out questions, matching the pace of her thumping heart.

"Reckon it's the Sheriff's? What's in it? Whose is it? Any cash?"

"There's cash, all right. Look!" Taylor said, handing the bills to Bobbi Leigh, who spread the notes in her palm.

Counting, Bobbi Leigh spoke in a rising pitch of astonishment, "One hundred, two hundred, three, twenty, forty, sixty, four hundred, twenty, seventy ...Wow! There's five hundred dollars here, at least! Identification?"

"Shush! *Whisper!* Don't ... see any," Taylor answered, thumbing through the wallet. "Amazing!"

"What's amazing, other than the obvious?" Bobbi Leigh asked, stacking the currency in ascending order of its denominations.

"This *wallet.* It looks *just* like my *Dad's,* a Broxton Royal, just like the one he-"

"Taylor! Do you think ...?"

"Shhh! Keep your *voice down.* I hear something. Someone's coming," Taylor whispered, "and I think I know who. Take the wallet and hide over there, behind that stone column!"

"I'm way ahead of you, Tay!"

Bobbi Leigh grabbed the wallet, shoved the fold of bills into her pocket, and dashed toward the far end of the room where she stooped behind a gigantic flowstone column with a cone-shaped base the diameter of a backyard swimming pool and taller than ten Bobbi Leighs. She killed her flashlight. Just then, Sheriff Hagan, along with Nimrod, emerged from the passageway.

"Um ... hello ... Sheriff Hagan ... sir-"

"Taylor Smart. So, you and Bobbi Leigh came back anyway, despite my specific instructions and warnings *not* to," the Sheriff said, wiping his hands on his pants.

"It's just *me*, sir. Bobbi Leigh was, um, too *chicken* to come here. I guess she knows you too well."

Bobbi Leigh heard Taylor's comment and wasn't sure whether to pounce out from behind her cover with a big "HEY!" or be thankful for the quick-thinking diversion. She wisely opted for the latter and bent lower to avoid casting bits of suspicious shadows from unwanted, probing light sources. She listened, hoping her pounding heart didn't give her away.

"You should have taken the advice of your friend," Sheriff Hagan said, scanning Taylor head to foot, as a hunter might size up his prey. "I thought I heard more than one voice in here. *You* moved these boulders all by yourself? You *are* quite the stout one, I suppose. Of course, the ground *is* wet, which probably helped you. Still ... I don't know. Are you sure Bobbi Leigh didn't help you? I don't take too kindly to liars!"

Sheriff Hagan examined the expansive space with a sweep of his flashlight, checking closely all the walls. Bats clung silently to rocky knobs. Water drops fell with a staccato rhythm, just as they had for countless years, leaving their mineral residue to harden ever slowly into timeless columns of stone, behind which stood Bobbi Leigh, as stiff as her cover. Taylor crossed her arms behind her and glanced toward the flowstone column.

"Talking to myself, I guess. Echoes, maybe. Those rocks weren't hard to move, really. Anybody could do it, even a *girl*. I'm no liar, Sheriff," Taylor said, the two fingers of her right hand crossed. "There's nobody else here. Why don't you give Bobbi Leigh's mom a call and see for yourself. By the way, have you noticed? The cave's *not* flooded, and there's no sign it will be. Isn't that *great!*"

Taylor Smart and the Chamber of Skulls

Taylor prayed the Sheriff did not call her bluff and phone Bobbi Leigh's mom.

"Ever the questioning rebels, you middle-schoolers! When will you learn to leave well enough alone and *submit* to your superiors? Well, no matter. In fact, your being here is rather ... how should I say it ... serendipitous."

'Serendipitous.' 'Serendipitous.' Taylor turned that word over and over in her mind. *Where have I heard that word before? Think, Taylor! That's* **right***, she remembered, it was used by Miss Peasy during the light bulb changing.*

Miss Peasy had mentioned how "serendipitous" it was that she had neighbors whom she could depend on to help with certain tasks best left alone by a woman of her "creeping age", as Miss Peasy phrased it, though in hindsight it seemed flying was yet another of those things best left alone by a woman of her "creeping age".

She said she had no one to turn to for such things until Mom and I came along. The timing of our being in the neighborhood was an **unexpected**

help *for Miss Peasy*, Taylor deduced. *How, then, is my being here in this cave an "unexpected help" for Sheriff Hagan?*

"Nimrod, let's take her back into the chamber of skulls. I'm *sure* she'll be very interested in the *surprise* we have for her. Oh, by the way, Taylor, you didn't happen to find a brown *wallet* lying around, did you? I seemed to have lost mine."

"Wallet? Why, no, Sheriff. What surprise?" Taylor asked nervously as Nimrod gripped her elbow and patted her pockets. Finding nothing, he jerked Taylor abruptly toward the chamber. "Ow! What's going on here?"

True to her nickname, Taylor offered firm resistance, once breaking free after slamming the point of her shoe toe into Nimrod's shin. That moment of fleeting freedom, coupled with Nimrod's angry screams of pain, soon dissolved as Nimrod managed to wrangle control of their captive, much to Hagan's amusement.

Taylor Smart and the Chamber of Skulls

Inside the dark chamber, Sheriff Hagan pointed his flashlight toward the floor.

"Almost had you there, Nimrod," Hagan said, laughing. Then he turned to Taylor. "Take a gander, my friend."

Taylor's eyes popped wide, and her jaw fell like sabotaged wheels from a plane.

"*Dad!* Oh my gosh, *Dad!*" Taylor screamed.

Bobbi Leigh clearly heard Taylor's shout but thought perhaps the cave's acoustics played tricks on her.

*Taylor's **Dad**, in the chamber of skulls? He's **alive? Here?*** Bobbi Leigh wondered, almost aloud. She had to look but dared not.

Bobbi Leigh's mounting curiosity, and the fact that Taylor was now a captive of none other than Sheriff Hagan, quite nearly forced her from the cover of her stone column, but she caught herself and listened for more.

Prodded by a series of nudges from Hagan's boot, Mike Smart began a slow stir from his unconsciousness. Mike rolled onto his back, lifting one knee, and rubbed his blurred eyes, trying vainly to wipe away the curtain of film.

"*Wake up!* You have a visitor," said Sheriff Hagan.

"Wha- ... visi ...? Who ...," Mike stammered.

"None other than your *very own daughter!*" replied the Sheriff as a grin of satisfaction crossed his face.

Mike reacted instantly, as if doused with a bucket of ice water. "Taylor! Where am-"

"Dad!" Taylor slumped to hug her dad, her tears soaking into his shirt. "They've put you in a cave!"

"Careful, Muley, or you'll ...you'll start a ... stalagmite right here ... on my shirt!"

Taylor laughed, releasing the tension of months of hopeful uncertainty, forgetting for a blissful second the predicament she now shared with her dad.

"Who's the mule *now*, dad?"

"Mule?" Hagan said.

"I thought you were ... *everybody* thought you were ... except Mom. She always believed."

Taylor lifted her head and gave Sheriff Hagan the angriest glare she could muster, realizing that, for all these months, *he* knew her dad was not dead.

"You!"

"Now, now, mustn't get all riled. What's done is done. Look on the bright side! Now you're together again – permanently!"

"You want I should ...?" Nimrod asked.

"Naw! Not yet. They surely have much to catch up on. Let them spend their last days together alone, in the coziness of this dark tomb." Sheriff Hagan managed a chuckle. "Now there's just Susan and Peasy to deal with."

Mike, upon hearing his wife's name and still fending off the effects of the sedative, tried desperately to rise to his feet. He stumbled, smacking his body against the damp rock wall, and slumped to the floor. Taylor rushed to cushion his collapse. Hagan and Nimrod laughed at the awkward spectacle.

"It was *you* who tampered with Miss Peasy's plane wheels! You tried to kill all *three* of us."

"That's right, you two, just talk. Like I said, lot's to catch up on. Yes, 'twas I who fiddled with the Witch of Raventon's wheels, but don't give me *all* the credit; Nimrod helped, too! I underestimated her skills, 'tis true. Oh, and you won't be needing this flashlight, Taylor," the Sheriff said as he yanked the light from her resistant grip. "Mustn't *waste* energy! Come, Nimrod. Time to position the boulders and bid our guests adieu."

"You can't just *leave* us here!" Taylor shouted. "*Wait!* What is it you *want* anyway!"

"Oh, but I *can* leave you here. And so I *shall!* By the way, Taylor, if you feel around very carefully, you might chance upon an arrowhead or two, perhaps a *skull*. Enjoy your prehistoric friends! Happy trails!"

26

Candles and String

"While no one is expected to leap tall buildings in a single bound, our aspiring heroes will be tested on their courage, integrity, self-sacrifice, compassion and resourcefulness - the stuff of all true superheroes."

- Stan Lee

That sinister parting spoken, the Sheriff and Nimrod departed the chamber of skulls and the large room preceding the tunnel connector. Bobbi Leigh remained stone silent behind the ancient column. She heard the sound of the men's garbled words and laughter as it dissipated in the growing distance and the barriers of rock. She smelled the putrid, lingering odor of Nimrod's second-hand smoke. She heard the men grunt with effort and curse with anger at each step and misstep as they pushed a huge boulder, perhaps two, their intent to block the narrow link to this part of the cave and forever seal that exit.

Then, silence.

Bobbi Leigh strained with unfamiliar focus, but she detected no sound from the direction of the cave's entrance room. After a few extra minutes, just to be sure, she concluded it safe for her to emerge.

"Taylor?" she whispered loudly.

"Bobbi Leigh! It's my *Dad! Get in here!*"

The light from Bobbi Leigh's SureShot bounced from wall to floor to ceiling and back as she dashed from the cover of her column shield, leaping over and sidestepping scattered stone obstacles in her race to the chamber of skulls.

Mike's sedative-induced stupor persisted, but he was regaining some cognizance.

"How'd you find ... Where am I? Is Susan-"

"Dad, we're in a *cave*, at Lake Jasper next to Tucker's Mountain. Sheriff Hagan brought you here. Where has he been *keeping* you this past year? We thought–the police, that is–thought you were ... dead! They even called off the search for you, and now I know *why!*"

"Taylor, how are we going to get *out* of here?" Bobbi Leigh shouted, her composure disintegrating. "I heard them pushing boulders – had to be big ones – over the passageway entrance. More than we'd *ever* be able to move crouched on our stomachs! They've left us here to *die*, Tay!"

"*Hush up*, Bobbi Leigh! Don't make me slap you!" Taylor said sternly, looking at her dad. "We're *not* the dying kind, right Dad?"

Mike managed a smile of acknowledgement.

Just then, Bobbi Leigh's SureShot flickered and dimmed.

"*Not again!*" Bobbi Leigh shouted, handing the flashlight to Taylor.

"Bobbi Leigh, I have *candles*, remember?" Taylor said, transformed to calmness by the presence of her living dad.

"Oh my gosh, *yes!* You brought *candles!* Girl Scouts sure make handy friends! The Sheriff didn't count on *that*, but ... how're *candles* going to get us out of here?"

"Well, without light, it's hopeless. We would just become another pile of bones. *With* light, even candlelight, we at *least* have a shot, even if it's not a ... *sure* shot. Do you hear that rushing sound?" Taylor asked, cupping her hand around her ear.

"Yes. That way," Bobbi Leigh said, pointing to a passage leading to unexplored areas of the cave.

"Could be the stream Hagan spoke of, maybe," Taylor speculated, shifting the dimming light toward the sound, "but it seems that, given the upward slope of the cave floor in that direction, an underground stream would be unlikely."

"Unless the slope turns *downward* beyond that passageway," Bobbi Leigh suggested. "Who knows how big this cave *really* is!"

"True. So, if it *is* the stream, it has got to go *somewhere!* They can't stay underground forever, can they?"

"What are you suggesting, Taylor?" Bobbi Leigh asked, worrisome skepticism lacing her voice.

"We can't stay *here*, agreed?"

"Agreed."

Mike had slipped back into unconsciousness.

"One of us has to follow that sound and see where it leads! It may be our only hope for getting out of here. Remember the Sheriff telling us he intended to seal this cave tomorrow!"

"But, your dad's asleep again. He's in no condition to move, Taylor, even if he *were* awake! One of us has to stay here with him, while the other follows the sound, with the light of the candles."

The SureShot dimmed further. Taylor's eyes connected with Bobbi Leigh's.

"How many candles did you bring, Tay?"

"Eight. Five stubby, fat ones that ought to last a while and three longer ones that pretty much do little more than dress up a dinner table and drip hot wax on your fingers."

"Hot wax beats cold stone any day!" Bobbi Leigh said, laughing. "So, um ... who's going?"

"Like you said, somebody's got to stay here with my dad. I'm thinking that somebody ought to be me."

"Yeah, but ... of course, Tay, you're right. I'll go. Let me have plenty of matches, maybe three of the stubby candles, and one silver bullet."

"Thanks, Bobbi Leigh. You're our silver bullet. And a *genuine* friend, like no other. I'm glad you stopped by my house at one thirty in the morning that stormy night."

"Seems like *forever* ago!"

"We thought you were pretty nutty, out that late, walking dogs in a thunderstorm, and with no parents home. Turns out you're the *coolest!* No *ifs, ands, or buts* about it!"

The girls laughed and gave each other a hug.

"Your *Dad*, Tay! You *found* your dad!" Bobbi Leigh shouted, grabbing Taylor's hands. "This is the most incredible thing I've ever witnessed! That, and five hundred dollars in cash. Why'd your dad keep that kind of money on him?"

Nodding her emphatic agreement, Taylor handed Bobbi Leigh the candles, matches, and something else.

"Always paid for everything in cash. Other than cars and mortgages, he never believed in credit."

"Oh, one of *those.* So, what's this?" Bobbi Leigh asked.

"What does it *look* like, silly!"

"A ball of string, kite string, but ..."

"You'll need to leave a trail, so you can make your way back, if need be. There are probably a couple of thousand yards of string on this ball. The sound seems closer than that, I hope. Leave a trail, Bobbi Leigh, and let's hope that you have more string than you have trail!"

"You think of *everything*, don't you?"

"My mama didn't raise no fool!"

Both enjoyed an adrenalin-fueled laugh.

"Miss Peasy's okay, isn't she?" Bobbi Leigh asked. "I mean, she's no witch."

"No witch, Bobbi Leigh," Taylor affirmed. "She's okay. Set in her peculiar ways, maybe, but she bakes the best apple pies I ever ate and she's the finest pilot this side of World War II. It's the *Sheriff* who's the *real* Raventon Witch!"

"Amen to that! Look!" Bobbi Leigh said, reaching towards her feet.

"Wow. Another arrowhead. You get *all* the luck!" Taylor smiled.

"Some *luck!*" Bobbi Leigh replied, handing the point to Taylor for safekeeping.

"It was pointing that way, towards the sound. I'll just bet the prehistorics knew another way out."

"I'm gone, Tay," Bobbi Leigh said as she scratched a match on the cave wall and touched it to the candle wick. "If I'm not back in a couple of hours, then assume I've found a way out and am going for help. Tell your dad we *will* get out of here."

"One more thing, Bobbi Leigh," Taylor said, reaching for Bobbi Leigh's backpack. She unzipped a side pocket and placed her hand inside.

"What did you put in there? Looked to me like just an empty hand."

"Couple of things, ideas actually, that always served me well when I needed them most."

"Okay. *So ...*"

"A bit of bravery and the right to be afraid," Taylor answered. "Mix 'em together and you've got courage. Not that you'll need any, but I wanted to give you some extra, just in case."

Bobbi Leigh patted the backpack pocket.

"Thanks, Taylor," Bobbi Leigh said with a smile, "but I've already got more 'afraid' than I know what to do with."

"Be careful, Bobbi Leigh," Taylor said, catching her words too late and rolling her eyes at how familiarly annoying that phrase sounded. "Take this sandwich and water. It's going to take you longer because of having to lay down the string, so watch your step. Take all the time you need! We'll be here. *Safety first!* And give mom the cash. No stopping at souvenir shops along the way!"

"Like you had to tell me *that?*"

Bobbi Leigh stuffed the sandwich and water bottle into her backpack. She loosened the end of the string from the ball, and, clutching it in her palm, gave Taylor a thumbs-up.

The girls exchanged smiles. Mike groaned.

Bobbi Leigh turned and disappeared into the blackness of the cave, an eerie glow of candle light bobbing and bouncing, fading, then vanishing.

Taylor watched and sighed, wondering if she would ever see her friend again.

Mark Randolph Watters

27

Phobia

"He has not learned the lesson of life who does not every day surmount a fear."

- Emerson

Bobbi Leigh Harwell, in her most far-reaching imaginings and daydreams of adventures, never pictured herself in the middle of a bat-ridden mountain cave, alone, the meager flicker of a stubby pillar candle the difference between the here-and-now and the hereafter.

She managed the awkward process of holding the string ball in her right hand, the candle in her left, and loosening the string with her teeth. She worked her way forward, a few inches of string falling with each step. An occasional glance behind convinced her that the string trail indeed served its purpose, a doubt she harbored as soon as Taylor mentioned the idea.

The rushing sound of water grew louder. Her candle flame held steady and surprisingly bright, the equivalent of several lumens! No hot wax dripped. Bats seemed more plentiful in this part of the cave, clusters of the critters visible here and there near the ceiling and between stalactites. The cave formations startled Bobbi Leigh with their magnificence of size and colors.

As Bobbi Leigh reached to release the string snagged in the crevice of a boulder, the candlelight caught the sparkle of a pink sugar quartz spear point nestled in a cup-like depression in the cave floor. She reached and picked it up, feeling its polished patina and marveling at its artistic lines and skilled symmetry. Their existence long gone from the cave, the evidence of an ancient Native American presence comforted Bobbi Leigh and helped her cling with relative reassurance to the thought that, though ages ago, humans had traversed these parts of the cave countless times.

Bobbi Leigh wedged the candle and string between twin stalagmites.

"This one's for Muley," she whispered as she carefully wrapped the point within a soft hand towel she kept inside her backpack.

The rocky terrain dipped and rose, like a grassless meadow. Bobbi Leigh struggled to climb over slippery flowstone and boulders, often having to balance the candle on uneven surfaces while she maneuvered over and around such obstacles. Amid her focus to navigate within the dangerous slivers of broken light, the string ball had shrunk dangerously small.

The rushing water sound had grown astoundingly loud–and close! Bobbi Leigh could see the shadowy curve of a bend in the passage ahead. Around that curve, she knew, resided the source of the torrent.

As Bobbi Leigh rounded the curve, her eyes were met with the mad tumble of the stream of water, probably 30 feet in width, she guessed, as it crashed wildly over boulders and against walls. Spray and splash from the water covered Bobbi Leigh's face. She tried with vain desperation to shield the candle flame from the ferocity of the flying drops.

The sound and sight, frightening in its overwhelming power and unknown magnitude, caused Bobbi Leigh to drop her candle, which rolled down a rocky embankment and into the thundering water.

In an instant, her panic was punctuated with a claustrophobic blackness. She froze stiff as ice, fearful of the possibility of following her candle into the water.

She arched her arm over her shoulder, toward the water, and pulled from her backpack the box of matches and a second candle, this one long. She struck the match along the matchbox side, producing a spark and a flameout. She scraped another, the stick snapping. Finally, after the agony of six failures, Bobbi Leigh touched fire to candle tip.

Keeping her back to the water and spray, she walked crab-like along the passageway, perilously parallel to the flow of the stream. This she managed for what seemed an eternity, slide-stepping her way through a surreal swirl of madness in hopes of soon finding that the stream exited the cave rather than plunging farther into it.

And exit, it did. Just ahead, around yet another excruciating bend, Bobbi Leigh glimpsed light not of her own making. The raging stream bent left once again, in the direction of the glow.

An exit! Bobbi Leigh thought, cuddling the last few meters of her string. *Finally, a way out!*

Around this last bend, Bobbi Leigh at last saw it. A huge opening in the cave wall and a blast of sunlight forced Bobbi Leigh to cover her eyes as they adjusted to the sudden change. She stepped closer to the opening, looking carefully between the fingers shielding her eyes. Water thundered through it, but, strangely, she saw no trees or forest or flowers one might expect to see along the banks of a mountain stream bathed with autumn sunlight.

This was because there *were* no banks of a mountain stream bathed in autumn sunlight. Bobbi Leigh inched her way forward, her pupils doing the dilation dance. Then, with a shock similar to sauerkraut on taste buds, she realized the doozie of the next step would not be that of soft grass of a mountain meadow.

Instead, the water transformed into the unforgiving drop of Sagitaw Falls! The falls exploded out of Tucker's Mountain and plummeted some 150 feet to a narrow, craggy shelf and beyond to house-sized boulders waiting at the bottom of its nearly five-hundred-foot plunge.

Terrified of heights, Bobbi Leigh forced herself to peer out the clear expanse beyond the falls at the mouth's edge, the point where the stream made its abrupt 90-degree drop. How was *this* a way out?

Taylor Smart and the Chamber of Skulls

It wasn't, Bobbi Leigh believed, until she noticed to her left a narrow strip of cave floor leading to a narrower strip of cliff ledge that appeared undisturbed by fallen rock and the flow of water.

Was this one of the ancient routes taken by Native Americans out of the cave? *Only one way to find out*, she thought, remembering Taylor's words. Finding out, she would soon find out, meant accepting a level of fear heretofore unknown to Bobbi Leigh Harwell.

Bobbi Leigh sucked in a chest full of air. Her heart beat like the feet of a tap dancer. She extended her left foot out onto the ledge, tapping it and pressing a bit harder each time as if to confirm the firmness of the ground. She hadn't fully seen the depth of the drop and didn't want to.

Bobbi Leigh thought it wise to leave her backpack behind. Its bulkiness hanging against her back took up valuable real estate. *Nothing worse*, she thought, *than to be forced to my doom by a stupid backpack!*

Though meant as symbolic encouragement, she remembered what Taylor had placed inside her backpack. Unzipping the side pocket, she withdrew its invisible contents, stuffing it into her pants pocket. As Bobbi Leigh leaned her backpack against the cave wall near the brink of the falls, she felt her fear rise more than ever before. *It's working!* She thought. *I certainly feel the right to be afraid!* The bravery, on the other hand, took its time.

Slowly, she slid a foot onto the ledge, then another, and froze. She pressed her back and hands against the cliff's side.

"I can't *do* this! C'mon *bravery*, do your stuff! It's time to make some courage!"

The ledge, from wall to drop-off, was little wider than the depth of the bookshelf in her bedroom. Bobbi Leigh sloshed into some muddy spots, at which she stopped cold to anchor her feet and to secure her next step. The least of her worries, cold water soaked her feet. The roar of the water fed the dread clawing to the surface in her mind.

"I've got no choice, do I?" she said, eyes closed. "I *know* you need me, Taylor, but ... one slip in this slime and I'm *toast!*"

She stopped and took a pair of deep breaths.

Bobbi Leigh's fingers clung to the slightest protrusions of rock as she made her way out of the cave and into the open air. Stepping from her claustrophobia into her acrophobia offered no comfort. A sudden, new phobia emerged, the phobia to end all phobias–thanatophobia, the fear of death. Regardless, she had no choice but to press on.

"Is this really happening?"

Bobbi Leigh liked asking that rhetorical question in times of special fun, fun that seemed during those magical moments too fun to be real, such as holidays; birthdays; and field trips. Now, reality took on a sudden nightmarish pall, a one-eighty she'd never before experienced.

Bobbi Leigh wondered if she might be visible to hikers below, and if so, if any of them had noticed her and realized the obvious absurdity of a person, a little girl, clinging to a cliff ledge adjacent to the chaos of Sagitaw Falls, and, well, while they were noticing, to send for help.

"I'm gonna fall, I just *know* it!"

"No, you're *not*, Bobbi Leigh! *Suck it up, girl!*"

"Oh my *gosh!* The water is so *loud!* I *can't* look!"

"You've *got* to look!"

"Okay, God, it's You and me and gravity. I'll swap my vertigo for steady legs and sticky shoes! And make it snappy! *Please?*"

Then the ledge widened a bit, maybe to a half meter, as if in response to a prayer, though Bobbi Leigh hoped for a more emphatic answer. The slope leveled, and she issued a sigh.

Still, as winds whipped around her and the growl of water filled her ears, fear continued its domination. Heights had a paralyzing effect on Bobbi Leigh Harwell, particularly rides in airplanes and elevators, though at least with those situations she was enclosed in a controlled unit of transport.

Here, she was exposed to the whims of every unforgiving, three-dimensional element; the changing directions of wind gusts; water spraying her face like the crash of waves on the rocks; the terrifying roar of the falls; and the merciless distance to the earth below. Bobbi Leigh was out of the cave, out of its suffocating darkness, but by no means was she out of the grip of danger or her fears. The blood driving through her veins felt like the pounding of the pistons of a diesel train. The bedlam bubbling inside Bobbi Leigh's brain felt like a churning din of madness.

The swirl of spray from all directions filled her immediate space as the force of the falls pushed outward into the surrounding air. Bobbi Leigh's thoughts swirled as well. Her mind ricocheted from the clear and present dangers, to Taylor and Taylor's dad; to Red Motor crops and how these were all but ruined; to the eccentricities of the emerald-eyed Miss Peasy; to what might be on the table for supper, should she make it home for supper, for *anything.*

She dared *not* look down, except for a tiny, irresistible squint. Not even Bobbi Leigh's phobias could prevent that!

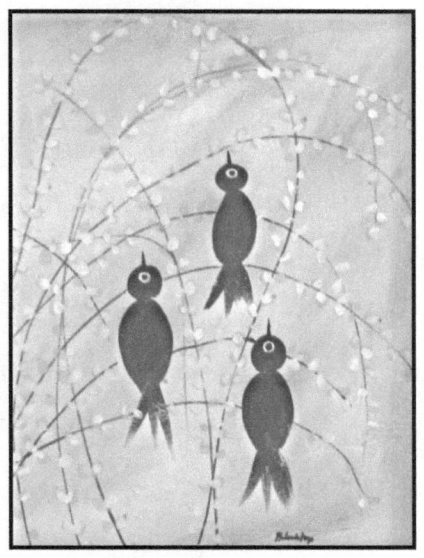

28

Reunited

"Speaks for itself."

- everyone

Taylor heaved an anxious sigh and squatted against the cold wall. She set the fat candle next to a boulder, the candle's light casting an eerie pirouette of shadow and glow throughout the chamber of skulls. Eyeless sockets peered back at her. The stories *they* could tell.

She reached up, trailing her fingers over a petroglyph, and wondered how her friend was faring in the depths of the unknown. Her dad again unconscious, Taylor thought of striking a conversation with the skulls, anything to pass the time. Were these the innocuous remains of Native American cave burials or evidence of something sinister? Mike stirred once again, and Taylor rushed to his side.

"Dad!"

Mike groaned in pained response to his throbbing brain. He lifted his torso and propped on his elbows. He managed to lean against the cave wall next to the outcrop lined with skulls. As he regained some focus of his eyes, he turned toward the line.

"AAAHH!" he shouted.

Taylor laughed. "That's what *I* said when *I* first saw 'em! It's like you're in the catacombs, eh, Dad? Say 'hello' to ten of my oldest friends!"

"What are ... are these ... skulls, Taylor, what-?"

"How do you feel, Dad?"

"Lousy. Headache ... weak," Mike said, rubbing his forehead. "What *are* those?"

"Not sure. My guess is they're remains from Indian burials. See these petroglyphs?"

"But the row of skulls suggests these heads were severed, which sounds like a pretty good idea for my ... aching coconut!"

Mike picked up a leg bone. He ran his fingers along its length and noticed a neat row of notches near the joint.

"See these?" he said.

Taylor looked. "Yes. What are they for?"

"I'm not entirely sure. An archaeologist could tell us. See the spacing and uniformity ... of these notches? My guess is they could only have been put there by a human, as opposed ... wow, feeling really woozy here."

"Here, Dad," Taylor said, removing a water bottle from her backpack, "drink some of this."

"Thanks, Mewels." Mike drank a few sips.

"You called me 'Mewels'."

"You'd rather I-"

"Mewels is good!"

"Anyway, as I was saying ... animal teeth marks could never have been so precise or uniform. Could be a form of ancient ritual or sacrifice, which might ... might explain the skull placements." Mike sipped more water. "Or maybe they're evidence of some prehistoric surgery, maybe probing to remove a projectile. Hand me one of those skulls, Mewels."

Taylor selected the middle skull and handed it to Mike. He turned it for closer examination.

"Yes, look! This skull has a projectile point lodged in its left side-rear."

Mike turned the skull so Taylor could see the trim, triangular projectile point, half in, half out.

"Here's another skull with a hole nearly big enough for my fist to fit. These may be the dead from battle. We'll have to get the university paleontologists and archaeologists up here to investigate."

"So you think they're prehistoric?" Taylor asked.

"No doubt. Whoa!"

"What, Dad!"

"Still woozy. Those guys fed me sedatives almost every day, in my food, my water, through injections-"

"But *why*, Dad? *Why!* What do they want from you, from *us*?"

"Sheriff Hagan is after the house, Taylor. It's a long story, but there's a questionable legal trail of disputed ownership that goes back years, decades. The city of Raventon had put the matter to rest long ago. Hagan didn't.

"I was the obvious obstacle, the latest in a series of obstacles, but he couldn't quite bring himself to get rid of me the old fashioned way. As much as it pains me to say it, I guess Hagan has a *smidgeon* of a conscience, ever so small. And that's why I'm here, alive, in this cave. Out of sight, out of mind, his intentions were to let the elements take care of me.

"A bigger question might be, what are *you* doing here?"

"Long story, too, Dad. Bobbi Leigh's gone looking for another way out of here. They've sealed the passageway we used to get in here from the main entrance, and the Sheriff says he's going to seal the cave permanently."

"Bobbi Leigh? Who's Bobbi Leigh?"

"A friend ... a *great* friend of mine. That's another long story. I'll tell you all about her over ice cream and a slice of Miss Peasy Parlevous's apple pie."

"Ah, Miss Peasy-"

"A *really* long story! Hey, you should know her, right? Great carpenter, pilot ..." Taylor paused. "I wonder how she's doing."

"Miss Peasy?"

"No, silly. Bobbi Leigh. Sheriff Hagan and his goon boy – Nimrod's his name – caught Bobbi Leigh and me in here. Well, more like just me. Bobbi Leigh hid, and they didn't find her. We had come to investigate all these bones we found yesterday, to look for clues. You know, the legend of Tucker's Mountain and the Witch of Raventon, all that jazz.

"The Sheriff and Nim-boy told us not to be going back here because of the big storm we had yesterday. He said they were going to seal the cave permanently, because of the danger of floods. Something odd about that, about *him*, so, naturally we came back anyway. Plus, we had found the skulls yesterday – can't let skulls go uninvestigated – so we hid our bikes in the vines and came inside for another look. Turns out y*ou're* the reason they didn't want us poking around."

Taylor gave Mike a smile of mischief.

"Aren't you glad I *disobeyed* an authority figure, Dad?"

"You've always been good about facing your fears, Taylor," Mike said in a futile attempt to sound authoritative, "but defying authority is something we've strongly discouraged."

"But, Dad ..."

"Taylor," Mike said, shaking off the intensifying tingles out of his awakening arm, "I would be incredibly insincere if I were unhappy that your curiosity brought you back to the cave. Let's just say you did the right thing for the wrong reasons."

Taylor thought for a moment. "I'm not in trouble, am I?"

"Trouble? Not at all, my precious daughter. It's just that ... parents aren't afforded the luxury of seeing things as black or white. Just remember that curiosity can be a good thing when coupled with a ... with a little common sense," Mike said, then asked, "How's Mom?"

"She's doing ... She's hanging in there, Dad. We moved into the house Friday. What a *fantastic* job you've done with it! Mom told me the house was your surprise for me. I *love* that surprise, Dad, but I have to say *this* surprise beats that one!"

Mike struggled with a painful laugh.

"Dad, everybody thinks you're dead. They stopped searching for you months ago, probably at Hagan's direction. Mom thought about giving you a funeral but couldn't bring herself to do it."

"Good for Mom!" Mike said with a smile.

"She pretends to have this "life goes on" attitude, but I know you're all she thinks about. Wow, is she ever going to be surprised! And it's Halloween!" Taylor said, hugging her dad.

Suddenly, Taylor pushed back from her dad and looked at him with moon pie eyes. "Mom!"

"Hagan!" Mike added, the realization complete, the dots connected.

Mike tried getting up but immediately collapsed, striking his forehead against the wall. Blood oozed from the cut.

"Give it time, Dad!" Taylor said, eyeing her candle and reaching into her backpack for a hand towel. "That's all we can do for now. And hope that Bobbi Leigh finds a way out of here."

Mark Randolph Watters

29

Phobia Conquered!

"A hero is no braver than an ordinary person, but she *is* braver five minutes longer."

- Emerson

She dared not look *up*, either. Height goes both ways, so Bobbi Leigh kept her eyes focused ahead, despite a crazy desire to look height straight in its tempting eyes.

The ledge widened more, so much so that Bobbi Leigh no longer relied on crab steps and was able to breathe easier. She walked a couple hundred yards along the cliff's gradually widening edge, when ahead she noticed three ropes attached to anchors and descenders and more ropes dangling from above. Bobbi Leigh knew just enough about rappelling and rappellers to know she was now in their midst, in hope's midst. She smiled.

Bobbi Leigh stopped at the ropes and knelt. *"Anybody down there!"* she shouted, eyes closed.

She heard chatter and laughter but could not bring herself to look over the edge.

"Can you *hear* me?" she shouted again. "Help!"

"We hear you! Coming up!" a voice shouted back.

Soon, three climbers clambered onto the ledge. Each was shocked to see before them a young girl.

"Hey! How did *you* get here? I *know* you didn't come from *that* direction," the astonished climber said, pointing in the direction Bobbi Leigh was moving. "This ledge ends around that bend;

the winds whip like a hurricane; and the drop is straight down, about five hundred feet. And you don't have any *climbing gear.*"

"I have *survival* gear, instinct anyway," Bobbi Leigh replied, realizing in that instant that bravery had been part of the mixture all along, that courage had triumphed in a moment least expected, that God had delivered. "I just followed the stream, and this is where it led."

"Stream? So *how'd* you get up here?" the first climber repeated. "How old are you anyway?"

"Twelve," Bobbi Leigh replied as she turned and pointed in the direction of the falls.

The climbers stared open-mouthed at one another, realizing they had been one-upped by a twelve-year-old. This was a way of skinning a cat not even *they* had desired to attempt.

"That's a *cave!*" a climber shouted, pointing. "That's the cave of *Sagitaw Falls*, girl! There's a *whole lot* of water coming out of that cave, and you're telling us you did just *that*, come out of that *cave?*"

Bobbi Leigh smiled and nodded with proud affirmation, aware she had not only faced head-on her dreaded dual fears of enclosed spaces and heights, and won, but she also had accomplished a feat seasoned climbers were loathe to try.

"But, *how?*" another asked.

"Don't want to think about it now. They tell me ignorance is bliss, and right now I couldn't be ... *blisser.* Get me down from here and take me home, please, and maybe I'll tell you how it's done!" a proud Bobbi Leigh replied, chin high.

The three climbers smiled and nodded in agreement. Bobbi Leigh's story was worth the price of an interrupted afternoon's climb.

Of course, Bobbi Leigh did not tell them the whole story, and she bent the truth on the part of the story she *did* tell. She did not want to risk having the climbers going to the police or telling someone who *might* go to the police. Not now. This was *still her and Taylor's secret*, their mystery, and if she were any judge of Taylor's resourcefulness, she and her dad were doing just fine. Bobbi Leigh's modified version took considerably fewer words to tell, but more than that, she was in *desperate* need of a restroom.

Mark Randolph Watters

30

Mistaken Identity

"To be yourself in a world that is constantly trying to make you something else is the greatest accomplishment."

- Emerson

Back home from the harrowing adventure of occupying a wheel-less plane during a belly-flop landing, Susan propped against the kitchen counter, a cup of tea in hand, and pondered the day, this Halloween day.

She loved hot tea, particularly Earl Grey and its variants, Lady Grey her favorite, its wrap-around comfort consumed on crisp autumn mornings and icy winter days or days that just struck her contrarily. The past year had been a contrary year, lots of hot tea having passed her lips. The soothing liquid gave her warmth in a world too often cold as iron.

The thought of another steaming cup of tea enticed her as she reached for the cabinet handle, but her thoughts turned instead to the attic. She figured now was as good a time as any to paint over the words found yesterday on the attic walls and to figure out how she might arrange furniture for her attic office.

She climbed the creaky steps to the second floor and up into the attic. It smelled of a recent painting, not unusual given the fact recent paint covered its walls. But Susan's eye was almost immediately drawn to the far wall, to her right.

There, on that wall, in more-recent-than-recent paint – a sickly, drooling, apricot colored paint – were these large-lettered words:

"GET OUT!"

"HE'S DEAD!"

Susan gasped, her hand covering her mouth. These words, these *sinister* words, weren't here the day before!

Who could ...?

Susan's mind raced.

On the floor lay scattered piles of wadded Zippy Burger wrappers, along with pieces of buns and the slime of smushed pickles! Dark splotches of goo covered the floor in the corner near the wrappers.

"*Miss Peasy!*" Susan whispered. "Miss *Peasy?*"

Then another surprise caught Susan's eye. In the same corner she discerned a shadowy, vertical line from floor to ceiling, as if a long, straight crack in the wall had formed.

Mark Randolph Watters

Drawing nearer, and careful to avoid stepping in the dark goo, Susan reached for the crack, which, to her greater surprise, was no crack at all!

The shadowy line opened the wall, much like a door ajar, and revealed a set of steps heretofore unknown to her. Backing away, Susan dared not walk the dark, downward spiral.

Unable to speak, Susan turned and started to close the wall door, when, in her periphery, she noticed part of a flat, rectangular object, a photograph, jutting from under a Zippy Burger wrapper.

She reached to pick it up and gasped at the photograph's subjects, Susan; Taylor; and *Mike!* Susan recognized at once that this was the same photograph Mike carried in his wallet and the *only* copy she knew existed.

Susan's glare shifted toward the attic window overlooking Miss Peasy's side yard. Anger welled in her eyes and replaced her nagging suspicion with gnawing certainty. Leaving the scene relatively undisturbed, with the exception of a handful of the Zippy Burger wrappers and the photograph, Susan raced downstairs, intent on confronting Miss Peasy Parlevous.

Susan grabbed her cell phone off the dining room table and shoved open the kitchen screen door, scattering a group of sparrows pecking ants off her patio.

Miss Peasy just happened to be picking fallen leaves from her side yard garden of pansies. Hearing the rapid shuffle of shoes across the walkway and lawn, Miss Peasy straightened her bent frame, clutching her hip.

"Mrs. Smart, I'm pretty sure my plane was sabotaged, and once I–"

"Don't you dare 'Mrs. Smart' me, you … explain *this!*" Susan screamed, thrusting a handful of Zippy Burger wrappers under Miss Peasy's nose.

"What, you don't like *Zippies?* Oh, must be some of my wrappers blew into your yard. I'm as sorry as sorry can be, Mrs. Smart," Miss Peasy said, taken aback by Susan's sudden shift in demeanor. "Here, let me take-"

"These didn't ... *blow* into my *yard*. They were *taken* to my *attic,* along with that nasty black stuff you're always chewing and spitting ... what *is* that stuff, anyway!"

"Mrs. Smart, I don't rightly know what you're talking about. The black stuff's just licorice juice. Can't swallow it, never could. Gives me a doozie of a stomach pain, but I *do* love how licorice tastes. So I chew on the stick and spit out the juice. Folks think I chew tobacco, but it's not so. Lot of things people think about me ain't so. Zippy Burger wrappers in your attic? Reckon your husband left 'em there?"

"Mike did *not* chew licorice or tobacco, Miss Peasy, and he would *never* have written ... *words* ... on a freshly painted wall, words painted with *that!*" Susan said in a quivering voice, pointing to a half-filled can of apricot-colored paint concealed behind the wall of pansies.

"So *that's* where that bucket went!" Miss Peasy said, relieved to find her missing paint. "Ain't seen that paint since last Tuesday. Thought I'd left it on the porch, but ... well, here 'tis!"

"Miss Peasy, are you aware of a hidden passage of stairs leading to my attic?"

"The ones that come out to your backyard over yonder? Yes'm, Mike put 'em in himself. That's the one thing I *can't* do, build stairs. Never could get the angles just right, you know. I can belly-flop a plane fair enough, but I can't put together stairs."

"So you've known about the stairs?"

"Sure have. Haven't *you?* Of course you have, else you wouldn't be asking. So just what are you getting at, Mrs. Smart?"

"You haven't been in my attic, then."

"Been in your *attic!* Why, I haven't been in *my own* attic, Mrs. Smart, in *twenty years!* Only steps I'll attempt to climb are the porch steps and maybe your porch's ... and Flossy's! Arthritis, you see. Blame stuff's ruint my knees. I sleep downstairs in my house and leave well enough alone upstairs. Ain't no telling how *thick* the dust is on the furniture up there! I don't rightly yearn to climb *another's* stairs."

Susan gazed for a moment into Miss Peasy's emerald eyes, searching for signs of deception. Seeing none, Susan cleared her throat and said softly, "Well, then ... who *has* been in my attic, eating Zippy Burgers, chewing licorice, and painting with your apricot paint?"

"Sounds like somebody's trying to be ... me," Miss Peasy offered.

Susan thought about the creaking sounds heard coming from upstairs the previous two nights.

"Either it's a group of very smart *squirrels*," Susan replied, "or it's someone who knows something about Mike's disappearance. I found this photo of our family in the attic, Miss Peasy, a photo *Mike* always kept in *his wallet.*"

"And, I'm beginning to suspect it's someone with a hankering to sabotage Cessna wheels! I know that picture, Mrs. Smart. Mike told me himself he had never taken that picture out of his wallet, except the time he did to show it to me. And he *hated* Zippy Burgers or *any* sort of fast foods. Why, he was a runner, a jogger, a health *fanatic.* Saw him running all the time, when he wasn't renovating.

"Sounds to me like someone's trying to pin me with his ... well, you know what I'm talking about, Mrs. Smart. After all, I *am* the Witch of Raventon."

"The *what* of Raventon! *Witch?* I know you're working some wonderful magic on your apple pies, best pies I've ever tasted, but *you,* a *witch?*"

Susan laughed at the absurdity of the notion but then realized Miss Peasy was not sharing the laugh.

All these years, Miss Peasy had been subjected to the ridicule and tease of her neighbors, of her town, of folks who never took a few minutes to dig beyond their prejudice, their sense of superiority and the eccentricities of a person whose unusual ways challenged their smug paradigms. A good person lived behind the outward frumpiness of Miss Peasy, just as good houses live behind wrinkled paint.

Susan smiled and gently held Miss Peasy's crooked, arthritic fingers as she looked upon the disheveled burlap bag of the weathered woman standing before her, necklaces of buckeyes and peppers dangling as proudly as if they were pearls; gray Spanish-moss hair bobbing in the breeze; one cheek bulging with licorice juice; and apple pie crumbs clinging to her apron like babies to their mama, her emerald souvenir-frog eyes sparkling in the sun, the same weathered woman who earlier this day had saved the lives of her and Taylor. Susan could hardly find the words sufficient for a proper apology.

"I overreacted, Miss Peasy. Please forgive-"

"It's okay, Mrs. Smart. I'm a tough old bird, really. Percival can tell you! When life gets me down, I just bake me some pies, take me a plane ride, and eat me some Zippies. Gotten pretty good at it, I reckon."

Mark Randolph Watters

31

Identity Revealed

Just then, shouts of a girl could be heard. Both turned in the direction of the shouts, now nearer and distinctly desperate, and hurried to the front yard. Cresting the hill a couple hundred yards up the street, a girl ran as fast as she could toward the two women.

"Mrs. Smart! *Mrs. Smart!*"

"It's *Bobbi Leigh!*" Susan said.

"She's hollering like the world's come to an end! Reckon what she wants!" said Miss Peasy.

Bobbi Leigh broke her dead run and stumbled into Susan's yard.

"Mrs. Smart!" Bobbi Leigh repeated, hands propped against her knees, keeping her bent, breathless body from collapsing.

"Bobbi Leigh! Get your air, sweetie. What *is* it? Where's Taylor? Has something happened?" Susan knelt beside Bobbi Leigh.

"Where to begin!" Bobbi Leigh huffed. "Mrs. Smart, me and Taylor ... Sheriff Hagan wouldn't let ... Mrs. Smart, your *husband* ... he's *alive!*"

"Bobbi Leigh, what was that you said? *Bobbi Leigh!* Where's Taylor! Is she still in the cave?"

Susan's heart pounded as she tried frantically to make sense of Bobbi Leigh's jumbled, unbelievable words. Good news? Bad news? Clearly something was very wrong – or, perhaps very *right!*

"Try again, Bobbi Leigh."

Bobbi Leigh took a few deep breaths, turned her head away and spat. She swallowed and looked into Susan's waiting, anxious eyes. Before she spoke, she reached into her pocket.

"Here, Mrs. Smart. I think you'll want this," she said, handing Susan a wallet.

Susan gasped. "A Broxton Royal, just like ...*Mike's wallet!* Where did you-"

"The cave, Mrs. Smart. This is yours, too," Bobbi Leigh said, still sucking air, as she pulled out a scrambled wad of wrinkled bills. "Five hundred and something dollars, from the wallet."

Susan took the money and, peeling the wad apart, sobbed and said, *"Mike!"*

"Mrs. Smart," Bobbi Leigh interrupted, "your husband is alive! Taylor's with him in the cave."

"The *cave!* How did you two find him? Why is he in the cave? Is Taylor-"

"Taylor's fine, Mrs. Smart. They're both fine, but we've got to get back up there with some help!"

"I'll call Sheriff Hagan," Susan said, reaching for her cell phone.

"No! Mrs. Smart," Bobbi Leigh shouted, grabbing the phone, "you must *not* call Sheriff Hagan."

"But ..." Susan said, stopping in mid-thought. She looked at Miss Peasy.

Bobbi Leigh looked into Susan's eyes and turned to Miss Peasy.

"The Sheriff's behind all of this, isn't he, sweetheart?" Miss Peasy said softly to Bobbi Leigh.

Bobbi Leigh nodded. "The Sheriff and a fellow named Nimrod. They've sealed the cave. Taylor and your husband are in there."

Miss Peasy had barely spoken these words when Sheriff Hagan, seeing the three crouched on the grass, pulled curbside, pretending to offer assistance.

"Mrs. Smart, we must *not* say a word to him about this. He must *not* know that we know," Miss Peasy said. "You, too, Bobbi Leigh. Don't give him *any* reason to suspect a thing."

"Everything okay here?" the Sheriff asked calmly, as if on a normal day's patrol.

Of course, Hagan hadn't known that Bobbi Leigh returned that morning to the cave with Taylor. He also had not known anything of the ordeal Bobbi Leigh had just endured in her escape. As far as Hagan was concerned, Bobbi Leigh had been unwilling to defy his terse instruction, just as Taylor had told him so in the cave, and that indeed she had biked home.

The Sheriff leaned out the driver's side window. "Bobbi Leigh, I'm glad to know you were *smart* enough to stay away from that cave. All this rain we've had, bound to be some high, fast water in there. In fact, I've decided to just ban all future entry into that cave, seal it for good. I've posted some "No Trespassing" signs around the cave and at the entrance. Tomorrow, I'm bringing in a bulldozer to push a few of those lakeside boulders up against the entrance, forever sealing it. It's for the best, don't you think?"

Susan nodded in hollow agreement. Miss Peasy smiled as she rested her hands on Bobbi Leigh's shoulders.

"That's a good ... a good idea, Sheriff," Susan managed while clearing her throat.

"Getting a cold, Mrs. Smart? Eyes look a bit watery, and that throat. Can't be too careful about that flu going around. 'Tis the season, you know. Anyway, how's Taylor? Probably inside playing video games or watching television. Kids these days, and with this great fall weather!" Sheriff Hagan feigned laughter and, as he waved, added, "Well, I'll see you folks later."

The three waited until the Sheriff's cruiser disappeared over the hill.

"Mrs. Smart, we *must* get back to the cave, *now!*" Bobbi Leigh urged. "We'll need several people to move any boulders they've placed in front of the passageway Taylor and I found. That's the passageway that leads to the chamber your husband and Taylor are *in.*" Bobbi Leigh pulled Susan's arm. "We can't waste–"

"Bobbi Leigh ... how is it *you're* not trapped in the cave?" Susan asked.

Frustration building, Bobbi Leigh blurted, "Long story! Now let's *go!*"

"Miss Peasy, I'm going with Bobbi Leigh to the cave. Can you call-"

"I'm on it, Mrs. Smart. I'll get the County Police and Fire Department out there."

"An ambulance, too, Miss Peasy," Bobbi Leigh suggested.

"Right! You two be careful! My guess is he'll be patrolling the cave and lake area more than anyplace else."

"Thanks, Miss Peasy. When this is over, dinner's on me!"

"And the pie's on me," Miss Peasy said, looking down at her mussed clothing, "but I bet you'll eat it anyway!" she added, releasing a guffaw that bounced from tree to towering tree, scattering birds and felling a few acorns.

Susan and Bobbi Leigh hustled to the car and sped off toward Lake Jasper. Ignoring a stop sign, Susan slid her car into a skillful left turn, which, upon completing, was answered with a wailing siren closing fast behind them.

"Good *grief!*" Susan muttered.

"Sheriff Hagan?" Bobbi Leigh asked.

"Could be. Pretend you're sick, *your stomach!*"

Bobbi Leigh curled into a groaning ball, face down, clutching her stomach.

"In quite a hurry there, ma'am. License and registration, please," the officer demanded.

Nimrod! Bobbi Leigh thought with a gasp that very nearly raised unwanted eyebrows. *He's a deputy?*

"I'm on my way to the hospital, officer. My ... my daughter here is *very* sick, her stomach!"

"Throwing up?"

"And how! Projectile; the worst sort. Could happen again *any minute.* Might be appendicitis. You don't want-"

"Here, ma'am," Nimrod said, dropping Susan's license and registration into her lap and waving both his hands, as if to shoo her away. "I reckon you better go. Have a nice day!"

Susan smiled at the effectiveness of her trickery, and, as she raised her window, said, "If I hear 'have a nice day' one more time ..."

Mark Randolph Watters

32

Happy Anniversary

"Love is the only gold."

- Tennyson

Bobbi Leigh shared her story as Susan drove to the cave.

"Right here, Mrs. Smart, park *here!*" Bobbi Leigh urged. "We'll *walk* the rest of the way, beyond that curve. Let's just hope the Sheriff's not up here on patrol."

Susan and Bobbi Leigh arrived before any of the help Miss Peasy had summoned.

"Do you think Mike's hurt, Bobbi Leigh? Did he look hurt?"

"He looked fine to me, just sedated. Mr. Smart's probably been gagged or drugged for a good part of the past year, Mrs. Smart. The ambulance is for Hagan and Nimrod! They're going to need it *more* than Mr. Smart! "

"I am *amazed* you were able to find your way out, *that* way, through the cave and down the cliff! Took *real* courage to go through that."

"Fear plus bravery equals courage, Mrs. Smart. Something another twelve-year-old shared with me. It was the scariest thing I've ever done," Bobbi Leigh confessed. "It'll make for a fine show-and-tell, at least the 'tell' part. Not gonna show it ... unless-"

"You can just *forget* that, young lady," Susan said sternly, followed by a smile.

"Moms!"

Just then, a county police car zipped around the curve and Susan's car and halted at the cave's entrance in a swirl of splatter and leaves. Susan and Bobbi Leigh smiled, seeing that help had arrived.

"Ma'am, pull your vehicle around the curve ahead, out of sight."

Following instructions, Susan eased her car forward over puddled potholes and fallen branches and positioned it beyond the line of sight from the cave entrance. The officer followed her.

"Get in, ladies!" the officer shouted.

"What? *Why?*" Susan replied.

"Just *do* it!"

Susan and Bobbi Leigh climbed through the opened door into the back seat. The driver pressed the accelerator, jerking the unseatbelted Susan and Bobbi Leigh against the seat and each other.

"What *gives*, officer?" Susan shouted.

The driver focused on positioning his car in a similar fashion as Susan's, off the road and out of sight, and stopped. He shifted the stick into 'Park' and turned to face the pair. It was only then that Susan and Bobbi Leigh realized that the front seat passenger was *Miss Peasy*.

"Sheriff Hagan's on his way to the cave, Mrs. Smart. We didn't want him to see you, and we don't want to scare him off. If your husband and daughter *are* in that cave, as Miss Peasy says-"

"They're in there, all right!" Bobbi Leigh assured the officer.

"Then we believe he's going to want to check them out," the officer continued. "The Sheriff's not one to leave well enough alone, if you know what I mean. He'll keep going back and periodically going *inside* that cave until he finally seals the main entrance."

"He's coming now?" Susan asked, fear in her voice.

"He'll be here in a couple of minutes, ma'am," replied the officer. "He told his dispatcher he was on his way. If he goes inside, I'm going to follow him as quietly as I'm able and confront him when the time is right."

"Don't forget your flashlight!" Bobbi Leigh advised.

"Got it right here," the officer said, holding up his SureShot.

"Hey, I got one of *those!* Bobbi Leigh shouted. "The batteries bite, though! All those lumens? Lemons!"

"Don't I know it!" the officer confirmed, smiling and winking.

Heads turned toward the crunching sound of crushed branches and leaves, of pebbles popping from underneath rolling tires, of splashing puddles of mud. Through thickets of laurel, the four saw the Sheriff's car stop and doors open.

Sheriff Hagan and Deputy Nimrod exited the car and pranced toward the cave like cat burglars moving from house to house, their heads turning side to side as if expecting trouble. Both disappeared inside the cave.

Bobbi Leigh described what the officer could expect once inside the cave, particularly the narrow passageway through which he would have to crawl with the silence of a kitten.

"Stay here," the officer instructed.

*Yeah, like **that's** gonna happen,* Bobbi Leigh thought with a roll of her eyes.

The officer waited a few minutes before going in. He listened for movements, making sure his own would not be detected. Hearing none after

Mark Randolph Watters

Hagan and Nimrod had cleared the few boulders from the passageway, he advanced with all stealth through the entrance room and toward the passageway. He entered on hands and knees.

Voices!

The officer stopped upon hearing the sounds, the front of his shirt soaked to his belly from the occasional need to slither like a snake. His back throbbed with the pain of each scrape and bump received while crawling on his hands and knees under the passageway's low, uneven ceiling. He listened to discern the words, interrupted only by the beating of his heart.

"Well, I see you've not tried to escape, not that you *could* escape," Hagan said smugly. "Which is curious, come to think of it; but then, no doubt you see the utter *futility* in such an effort. Smart, I just wanted to ease your mind that Susan is fine. No harm will come to her, as long as she, you know … *cooperates.*"

"Why, you miserable–"

"Nimrod, please call this meeting to order," Hagan said with calm indifference, picking loose, dead skin from callused patches on his hands.

Nimrod pushed Mike, weak still from the lingering effects of sedation, to the floor. Taylor rushed and knelt at his side.

"Why are you doing this, Hagan?"

"Why *not?* It's *such* a lovely day for mischief, don't you agree?" Hagan retorted with a loud laugh. "Or, maybe because I *can!* Oh, okay, I'll give you the real answer, not that you knowing matters a wit."

The officer used the sound of Hagan's vociferous overconfidence to inch forward, knowing his presence, any other human presence, was the last thing Hagan and Nimrod expected. Behind him, he detected the shuffle of hands and feet, of Bobbi Leigh and Susan.

"If it's our house you're wanting-"

"*Your* house? Don't make me *laugh!* That house, kind sir, and all the gold hidden within its walls, belong to *me!*"

"*Gold?* So *that's* it. You're *crazy!* There's no *gold* in those walls! Just rumors passed down like bad colds."

"*Confederate* gold, Smart. Placed there long ago by one of your ancestors, Colonel Henry Smart, after he returned from the war. Hid it well, I might add. No one's ever found that gold, not a trace, and believe me, short of tearing the place down, folks have *tried!* But I *will* find it, every last shiny bar.

"Now if it were Confederate *currency* the good Colonel had hidden, I wouldn't give two hoots to find it, and you could *keep* your old house. But, gold is gold, no matter where it came from. So, yes, it *is* the house I'm wanting because it's the *gold* I'm wanting, because both belong to *me.*"

"To *you?* How do you figure that, Hagan?"

"Some legal paperwork foul-ups and such. It's no longer of any concern to you, Smart. Nimrod, cuff and gag them!"

Nimrod did all too well as he was told, the hastily fastened cuffs chewing into their wrists.

Taylor Smart and the Chamber of Skulls

Meanwhile, the officer, Susan, and Bobbi Leigh had completed their crawl through the passageway and had quietly stood up in the great room out of sight from Hagan and Nimrod.

"We'll be going now, Mike Smart. We're leaving you with this lighted candle. I know, I know, even *I* have a soft spot," Hagan teased, pressing his hand to his heart. "Just think, you'll forever be with the Natives who first occupied this cave. Who knows, maybe someday some archaeologist will stumble upon *your* remains, and after a carbon dating, will be *baffled* by the difference in age. What a legend *that* will spark! Oh, and thanks for the renovations! Top-notch job! Let's be off to our party, Nimrod."

With that, Hagan turned and met face to face the ones who would spoil their party. Shocked stiff, the Sheriff dropped his flashlight. The officer seized the opportunity to grab Hagan's service revolver from its holster. Nimrod threw down the handcuff keys and dashed for the passageway leading to the part through which Bobbi Leigh had earlier blazed, toward the rushing sound.

"Don't worry about him, sir! Believe me, he won't get far," Bobbi Leigh assured the officer.

"Bobbi Leigh!" Taylor shouted, having managed to push aside with her tongue the loosely applied cloth gag. *"Mom!"*

"Oh my gosh, Taylor! *Mike!*" Susan shouted, overwhelmed by her disbelief of this utter turn of circumstance and by her sheer joy. She rushed to his side.

"Careful, Mom, he's still weak," Taylor advised. "The handcuff keys are over there, by that flowstone!"

Susan retrieved the keys and quickly removed the cuffs. Not wanting to aggravate any injury, Susan examined Mike head to toe, assessing his general physical wellness. Then, with all abandon, she threw her arms around him and squeezed him as would a python, only more lovingly.

"I guess this means you didn't remarry," Mike said with deadpan stoicism.

"Not on *your life*, sir Mike-o-mine!" Susan answered with a kiss.

The officer reached for his handcuffs. Just as he clicked one cuff to Hagan's right wrist, Hagan bolted for the same passageway through which Nimrod ran.

"Stop!" shouted the officer as he realized how dumb *that* must have sounded.

"What's it like through there, Bobbi Leigh?" the officer asked.

"Dark ... and loud, and it'll get *really* wet for them *really* soon! But they're in for an even *bigger* surprise," Bobbi Leigh said with a laugh.

"*What*, Bobbi Leigh! Where does the cave exit?" Taylor asked.

Bobbi Leigh just grinned.

"Let's *go*, Bobbi Leigh!" the officer instructed.

Taylor and Bobbi Leigh followed. Susan and Mike stayed behind, enjoying Taylor's sandwiches and sipping her water. The flame of a stubby candle flickered and danced.

"Waiter, more wine, please," Mike said in his haughtiest tone, raising the water bottle in toast to the sightless stare of their skull company. Susan laughed and cuddled closer.

"What date is it, Susan?" Mike asked.

"The thirty-first."

"... *of* ...?"

"...of *October*, silly!" Susan said before remembering that Mike had not been in any condition to watch calendars. With raised eyebrows, Susan smiled slyly and announced, "It's *Halloween!*"

"Not *exactly* the answer I'd *hoped* for," Mike said, "but ... *happy anniversary!*"

"It's *exactly* the answer I'd hoped for," Susan replied.

33

Chamber Music

"Music is what feelings sound like."

- unknown

"This must be your string, Bobbi Leigh," the officer said, noticing the trail put down. "Well done!"

"Credit goes to Taylor, sir. She's the brains of this outfit!"

"Then kudos to you, too, Taylor! What's up ahead, Bobbi Leigh, what sort of surprise you

spoke of? I can hear them shouting at each other."
The officer stopped and listened. "Cover your ears,
girls! Such language isn't for twelve-year-olds."

"Heard worse, sir," Bobbi Leigh said. "Hear
that sound of rushing water? Of *course* you do,
silly me! Anyway, that's *one monster of an
underground stream*, only it's not your *ordinary*
monster of an underground stream, especially after
these rains. It turns into Sagitaw Falls and gushes
out of this cave like Niagara! It's a straight-down
drop of, oh, I don't know, a *million feet* or so!"

"So *this* is where that waterfall comes from,"
the officer said with a sense of amazement, hands
on hips.

"Yes sir! And those two're either going to
have to jump or get arrested. My money's on
arrested!" Bobbi Leigh shouted.

"But, Bobbi Leigh, how ... how did *you*
manage to get out! You weren't arrested, and you
didn't jump." Taylor asked, stopping dead in her
tracks.

"Took up rappelling at the last minute!" Bobbi Leigh answered, as easily as if she'd been asked the capital of the United States of America. "Found that bit of that courage you talked about, too. Thanks."

"Rappelling? I thought you and heights were bitter enemies!"

"Like I said, *courage*. Me and heights *were* enemies, and we're *still* not exactly on speaking terms, but I managed to get myself onto a very narrow ledge to the left of the waterfall. I was so scared, my fingernails were biting *themselves!* Made it along the ledge a while, too afraid to look down, and then I saw some climbers' ropes hanging over the ledge, and well, *here I am!*"

Here she was, indeed. But where were Hagan and Nimrod?

"This must be Sagitaw Falls, Sheriff!" Nimrod shouted above the watery mayhem. "There's a ledge ... over here, if I can ... just get ... my foot ... AAAHHHH!"

"That'll do, Hagan!" the officer shouted. "Hands on your head!"

"But, Nimrod ... he ... let me just look out-"

"Back away from the ledge, Hagan."

"I say *push* him on out, officer!" Bobbi Leigh shouted, "like he *just* did to Nim-boy!"

Taylor was inclined to agree but held her tongue.

Bobbi Leigh reached into her pocket and pulled out the taper-stemmed, yellow-tipped projectile point found the previous day in the cave, its milky white quartz glowing pure as sugar against her palm.

"This is yours, isn't it, Sheriff?" Bobbi Leigh asked, holding up the point between her index finger and thumb. "Found it in the cave yesterday. Thought I was the first person in thousands of years to handle it. Then I remembered *you* showing me one just like this–*exactly* like it, yellow tip and all–and well ... there *aren't* two points *exactly alike*. I've always wanted to own a beautiful piece of prehistory, and *luckily* I found this other one today, back up the path a piece."

She gazed closely at the yellow-tipped point, turning it carefully in her hand and admiring the magnificence of its ancient art.

"I've a mind to keep this point, too, to help me remember what a *slug* you are, what a *day* this has been. But, I don't really want to remember you. Keeping this reminder would be an insult to the beauty of prehistoric Native American artistry. So, this is one left-behind I can do without."

Bobbi Leigh held the point in her hand, arm extended, as if to hand the point back to Sheriff Hagan. But as Hagan reached to take it, Bobbi Leigh flung the projectile as hard as her Little-League arm allowed. Hagan gasped. The point splashed imperceptibly into the brink of the churning falls, forever returned to its rightful place in prehistory.

"I'm curious, Hagan," Bobbi Leigh observed. "Not that it matters now, but why didn't you take the cash from Mr. Smart's wallet?"

"I may be a kidnapper, but I'm not some ... *thief!*" Hagan shot back.

"What's the difference?" Taylor noted.

The officer cuffed Hagan's left wrist, and the four began the walk back, past the roar of Sagitaw Falls and the wild stream that fed it, past cave formations unseen for hundreds of years until today, past clusters of bats, past a trail of kite string, past artifacts meant never to be found, to the chamber of skulls.

When they emerged from behind the flowstone column and into the chamber, like returning warriors, Mike was standing and walking, weak, but able to move on his own.

Susan shone a flashlight on the group and then directed the beam fixed straight into the eyes of the cuffed Hagan. Hagan winced and turned his head, as would a vampire at dawn's rising.

"Y'all in there?" squealed a seasoned voice, that of the former Witch of Raventon, Miss Peasy Parlevous, from the cave's entrance chamber. "Somebody *talk* to me!"

"We're here, Miss Peasy," Taylor replied, leading the pack through the narrow, tube-like twist of a passageway. "Everybody's okay; just give us a few minutes!" She quickly re-thought and tried again. "Perhaps not *everybody*, but certainly the ones who matter!"

"Good, *very good!* I got me a handsome fireman here, ready if need be!"

"Can *always* use a handsome fireman, Miss Peasy," Susan shouted. Mike squeezed his wife's arm. "But, the only fire in here is an eternal flame," she turned to Mike and said. "Can't go putting *that* out!"

"I was hoping you'd say that, Mrs. Smart!" Miss Peasy shouted shrilly, clutching tighter the fire fighter's arm.

"Aww! They're so *cute!*" Taylor gushed, watching her Mom and Dad cling to one another and thinking what a sight Miss Peasy and the fireman must be.

"Grownups! Like a couple of *kids!*" Bobbi Leigh said, shaking her head.

Emerging into the cave's entrance room, the group helped each other to stand.

"Speaking of kids," Mike asked, wiping the coagulation of blood from his head bump, "who wants to hear a joke?"

"Da-a-a-a-ad!" Taylor said, rolling each letter to a whiny pitch.

"No, really, Mewels, you'll *love* this one!"

Bobbi Leigh glared at Taylor. "Mewels?"

Taylor squinted. "Here it comes, Bobbi Leigh."

"Okay, what do you call a group of Jack-Chi dogs from Monterey?"

"Where's Monterey?" Bobbi Leigh asked. "And what in the wide world of sports is a Jack-Chi dog?"

Taylor leaned and whispered into Bobbi Leigh's ear, "Don't complicate things! Just play along!"

"Oh. I-I don't know, Mr. Smart."

"Want to give it a shot, Taylor?" Mike asked, a Cheshire grin spanning his face. Susan checked her nails.

"Gee, Dad, I don't know. What *do* you call a group of Jack-Chi dogs from Monterey?"

"Monterey Jack-Chis!"

"That's a real hoot, Dad! Can we go now?"

"Got one more. Why does a milking stool have only three legs?"

Susan smiled at Taylor, each knowing they could do no more than wait this out. After all, Mike had waited a year for this moment.

"Give up? Because the cow has the udder! Get it? The ... **udder.**"

Silence. Deep, dark, bats-in-your-ears, cave silence, the worst kind.

"Ahem ... So, Bobbi Leigh, where's your backpack?" Taylor asked, thinking quickly.

"But that joke was *good!* Right? Wasn't it?"

"Dad, you and Miss Peasy were meant for each other!"

Mark Randolph Watters

Bobbi Leigh reached and patted her back. "Oh, *man!* I left it ... by the *falls* ... in the *cave!*" She pondered the ramifications of that thought for a second, then decided, "It ... it can wait."

"Want you to have this, Bobbi Leigh," Miss Peasy said softly, handing Bobbi Leigh her carved walking cane. "It was carved by a Cherokee and given to my great-great granddaddy back in 1836, at the beginning of the removal. That Cherokee told my great-great granddaddy he no longer needed it, that he'd rather die in the Georgia hills than walk to Oklahoma; well, for different reasons, I don't need it either."

Bobbi Leigh stared, mouth open.

"Miss Peasy, your *cane!* Why are you giving ... don't you *need* it?" Bobbi Leigh asked, gently grasping the hand-worn carved owl's head atop the cane and giving a close inspection of the other animal carvings that adorned the shaft.

"Need it? Nah. Got lots more of 'em. Walking sticks, that is. More'n I need, I 'spect. You've had your eye on this cane for quite a while,

Bobbi Leigh, and, well, I want you to have it. Go on, now, take it. After today, all I need to keep me upright are my new friends. Actually, walking never *felt* so *good!*"

Taylor reached to touch the cane. *"Lucky!"* she whispered.

"As for you, my flying friend, I'll spare you the bad jokes, but please take this," Miss Peasy said, glancing at Mike as she removed her necklace of dried buckeyes and shriveled banana peppers and handed the strand to Taylor.

"My daddy made me this very necklace when I entered the Army Air Force back in '42. Said the 'V' shape – for 'Victory' – it made hanging on my neck would bring me luck. I told him I wouldn't need no luck, that I was *born* lucky. The luck, I reckon, was more for *him* than me. Anyway, right as rain, he was. I've always had more than my share of … luck. Except I call it blessings, not luck. It's the blessing of a parent's *love*, not luck, what keeps a child going … an' going. You can call it whatever you want, Taylor, but I s'pect you agree with me. It'll go quite well with your arrowhead necklace."

"*Projectile point* necklace." Taylor cleared her throat. "Thank ... thank you, Miss Peasy." Taylor lowered Miss Peasy's gift around her neck, its length long enough to contain the projectile point necklace within its long oval, as if to protect it.

"Now," Miss Peasy squealed, slapping her hands, her emerald-green eyes asparkle, "who wants *apple pie!*"

"Now that *can't* wait!" said Taylor Smart, clutching both strands around her neck and rubbing her tummy.

Susan and Mike, Taylor and Bobbi Leigh, and the incomparable Miss Peasy ambled with rapturous leisure out of the cave at Tucker's Mountain.

Making their way towards the hidden vehicles, spurts of chatter and giggles alternated. Hagan grumbled, vowing now and again in an inaudible, whispering voice, to get his revenge.

Taylor Smart and the Chamber of Skulls

The officer opened the front-seat, passenger-side door for Bobbi Leigh. But, before she sat down, she turned to Taylor and, resting one hand upon her shoulder, looked squarely into her eyes, and with furrowed brows asked this question in a bone-dry tone only Bobbi Leigh Harwell could conjure.

"So, Muley ... how was *your* weekend?"

Mark Randolph Watters

"Tis the good reader that makes the good book."

- Ralph Waldo Emerson

**Thank you for reading Book One of the Raventon Mysteries, *Taylor Smart and the Chamber of Skulls.*
I sincerely hope you enjoyed it!**

Coming soon ...

Blythington's Game

The Raventon Mysteries

featuring Taylor Smart

Mark Randolph Watters

About the Author

Mark Randolph Watters
mark.watters@vikings.berry.edu

About as hum-drum a fellow as you'd ever want to meet, Mark finds his greatest satisfaction in time spent with his beautiful wife and daughter. Nothing in particular about Mark that the public might find extraordinary. In fact, he exudes 'ordinary'. He's not won the Pulitzer, nor has he been awarded the Newbery, nor has he held in his hands any Emmys , Oscars, or Tonys; he's not held public office, nor donated body parts to science (yet), nor made the talk show circuit. He can't sing (except badly). He won't EVER meet royalty, nor will he have his own reality show! He has, however, done greater than any of that – he's a stay-at-home Dad wholly devoted to his daughter's stable upbringing and well-being and to his wonderful wife. Who could ask for anything more?

More tidbits: Graduate of Berry College, Rome, GA; accounting background (did he say "hum-drum"?); passionate about the arts and writing (probably the most overlooked of the arts); winner of the Dahlonega Literary Festival Short Story Contest, both 2005 and 2006; author of two previous mainstream novels and seven children's picture books.

Mark Randolph Watters

About the Illustrator

Ken Gentle
a self-taught contemporary artist

See more of Blacktop's work at
www.blacktopfolkart.com

Alabama native and Rome, GA resident, **Ken Gentle** is a self-taught fulltime artist who began painting at an early age as a way of sharing his experiences of growing up in the South. Over ten years ago he began creating mixed-media paintings that include water colors, chimney soot, enamels, and acrylics. These paintings typically start with a base of "black tar" on wood, tar paper, tin or cardboard (hence the moniker "Blacktop"). His style of using a mixture of found objects further complements the stories he tells.

In addition to his studio in Rome, GA, Blacktop's works can be found at The Art House located in Buckhead, GA (www.thearthouseatlanta.com); Jeanine Taylor Folk Art in Sanford, FL; Wild Oats and Billy Goats in Decatur, GA; and many other galleries. Moreover, some of Blacktop's works are in the permanent collections at Appalachian State University and Kennesaw State University.